BOOK ONE

USA TODAY BESTSELLING AUTHOR

BROOKE O'BRIEN

BRIX

USA Today bestselling author Brooke O'Brien delivers a sizzling enemies to lovers romance where a snarky brunette has it out and falls in love with her high school bully turned stepbrother.

Brix Ward is a Grade A prick.

He's arrogant, spoiled, and self-centered. As the lead singer of A Rebels Havoc, he's used to women falling over themselves for a chance to tame the wild bad boy.

Except for me.

I still remember the boy I grew up with. The one who went out of his way to make my life a living hell. I did my best to avoid him at all costs.

Imagine my surprise when our parents announced they had eloped, then left me to live with my new stepbrother. Alone.

Now, no matter what I do, there's no escaping him. He's always there, tempting me, provoking me. Every moment of every day. The more we're around each other, the more the heat between us begins to rise.

If he thinks he can hurt me again, he's dead wrong.

I won't let him be the one to destroy me, even if it breaks my heart.

Thank you for reading **BRIX**! I hope you love Brix and Ivy story as much as I do.

You can join my Facebook group, Brooke O'Brien's Rebel Readers Group, to discuss the series and get sneak peeks on future releases. Sign up for my newsletter to find out more about my new releases. To join, visit: www.author-brookeobrien.com/brix

Happy reading!

DEDICATION

To every woman who's been done wrong by a man.
Keep your head high and your middle finger higher!

CHAPTER ONE

IVY

"I'll take a whiskey. Neat."

"You got it!" the bartender shouts over the music.

My eyes scan over the crowd of people packed into Whiskey Barrel Saloon, searching for any sign of my friend. She promised to meet me here after she got off work.

I rolled into town less than an hour ago. The moment I saw the "Welcome to Carolina Beach" sign passing into the city limits, I contemplated pulling over on the side of the road and turning the car around, convincing myself there had to be another way out of this.

Returning home for the summer had been last on my list of options, but in the end, it was for the best. My scholarship covered the first two years and it had been rough balancing a job with a full class load last year.

My mom raised me as a single parent since I was five when my dad took off out of town. He never even bothered to look back. She's done her part in raising me, and I hated the thought of relying on her. All I needed was a place to stay for the summer. I'd work, save up the money, and get my ass back to Chapel Hill to finish my last year as a Tarheel.

When I saw the band A Rebels Havoc printed across the flyer on the door, the deal was sealed. I knew this was a huge mistake.

"Here ya go." Placing a napkin on the counter, the bartender set the glass down in front of me.

So, here I was, back home for the summer, waiting for Kyla to show up. Once I saw the flyer, I immediately knew why she asked to meet here tonight. I can't blame her for not telling me sooner. If I knew A Rebels Havoc was going to be playing, I would've come up with an excuse as to why I couldn't make it.

I spot Kyla's brother, Madden, duck through the door, causing a knot of unease to coil tighter in the pit of my stomach. Not at all because of Madden.

It had everything to do with the guy walking through the door behind him.

Some things never change.

If only there were an eject button, some way to get me the hell out of here undetected.

Brix was dressed in all black, from the baseball cap on his head to the t-shirt fitting him like it was tailor-made for him, to the black denim jeans molding to his body in all the right ways. Even from here, I can spot the thin, silver chain hanging around his neck. My eyes roam over the dark ink covering his left arm while he makes conversation with the bouncer, his dark eyes searching over the crowd.

"There you are!" Kyla yells, as I glance over my shoulder.

She's gorgeous, her lavender-colored hair styled in curls pulled away from her face with a black choker wrapped around her neck. Her lips are painted a fire-engine red, and I'm starting to feel like I underdressed in my denim shorts, black tank top, and black espadrille sandals.

"Hey, girl." I smile at my friend, wrapping my arm around her for a hug.

"I'm so glad you're home." She bounces on her feet, clapping her hands. As much as I'm happy to see her, I wish I could say the same for myself.

"I didn't know your brother would be playing tonight."

Maybe it's the forced smile on my face or the sudden realization of the tidbit of information she forgot to share with me about tonight, her head turns away from me, eyes searching through the crowd. Mine follow along with hers until we both spot the guys near the front of the bar by the stage.

"If you don't want to stay to watch them, I understand."

"It's fine."

I'm not going to let him push me out of here. He's gotten away with embarrassing me and making me uncomfortable, to the point I'd take off running.

I'll be fuckin' damned if I let that shit slide again.

"Let's go find a table," she suggests while pointing her thumb over the wall wrapped around the side of the bar lined with booths. The name, Whiskey Barrel, fits the rustic feel. It's all weathered wood and iron beams.

Swiping my drink off the bar, I motion with the glass for her to lead the way. We find an empty booth near the front, which happens to also be close to the stage.

"Hey," Madden says, approaching us. "I had no idea you were going to be here tonight."

Madden's eyes bounce between his sister over to me. His narrow, trying to place me.

A lot has changed over the years. I'm not the same girl I was when I left Carolina Beach. Living on my own for the first time in my life forced me to learn a lot about myself. I found a voice, a confidence I didn't have when I was stuck in this hellhole of a town, and a style that suits me. I wasn't exactly the definition of pretty and popular back in high school. I've come a long way from my pimply face, oversized hoodies, and baggy jeans.

"Who's this?" Madden points to me.

"What the hell, Madd? It's Ivy."

Madden's eyes widen in recognition. They do a quick sweep of my body, as if seeing it for the first time, before finally meeting mine again. His mouth drops slightly, shaking himself from his thoughts, before he grins.

"Wow, Ivy. I didn't even recognize you."

He reaches his hands toward me, giving me a casual hug. When he steps back, I eye his black t-shirt with A Rebels Havoc printed across the front. His backward plaid hat paired with his well-kept beard gives off lumberjack vibes.

When I was in high school, I would often stay over at Kyla's house on the weekends. She was the closest thing I had to a sister, having grown up an only child. Madden took on the role of the pseudo big brother, looking after and protecting both of us.

Even when his band of dimwits came around, he would always keep an eye on us, threatening to knock some sense into anyone who didn't leave us alone. He'd never let anybody fuck with his sister, and I was thankful I was included in that, too.

"You look so... grown-up?" he mutters, bewildered. "Different... but in a good way."

"You ready to set up?" Brix interrupts. He may be the bane of my existence, but he's still one of Madden's best friends. He claps Madden on the shoulder before his eyes stop, falling on me.

I knew the moment Brix looked at me, the way his eyes did the same once-over Madden's just had, he didn't recognize me either. The only difference in how Brix looked at me was the not-so-subtle way he bit his lip before rubbing his hand over his chin, enjoying his blatant perusal of my body.

All the memories of him making fun of me growing up flash through my mind like a highlight reel of my high school years.

To say I hated Brix Ward would be a mild understatement. If he were to go up in flames standing in front of me, I wouldn't bother to offer him the glass of water in my hand.

"Yeah, man," Madden grunts, slapping him on the chest. "Give me a sec to grab a beer, and I'll be ready."

"I need a drink, too. I'll come with you," Kyla echos. She eyes me nervously, her eyes flash over to Brix, hesitant if she should leave us alone. I nod my head toward the bar, assuring her it's alright, I've got this.

"Be nice," Kyla jests, smacking Brix on the chest.

He has the nerve to act wounded, rubbing his hand where she had touched him, shouting over the music toward her asking, “What the hell was that for?”

I roll my eyes, taking another sip of whiskey.

“What’s your name, sweetheart?”

The words roll off his tongue, and I don’t hold back my cringe of disgust. Is this how he picks up women?

“Not interested.”

“Oh, really.” He laughs. He glances around us, checking to see if anyone may have overheard, before looking back to me. “Are you sure about that?”

“Oh, trust me,” I chuckle, “I’m very sure.”

"Is this some sort of hard-to-get move? ’Cause I happen to like a chase, but you should know, I always get what I want in the end.”

My eyes widen, nodding my head at his audacity. I’m afraid if I roll my eyes any harder, they’ll end up rolling out of my damn head. Does this garbage actually work on women?

Who am I kidding? Of course, it does.

I’m not blind to the heated stares blazing into him, eating him up like he’s some sort of sugary piece of eye candy.

I’ll admit it. He’s not bad to look at if you’re only looking at his appearance. If he hadn’t been the sole reason for making my life miserable years ago, I might even be able to overlook the fact he’s a player who’s looking to score and give in to his advances for one night.

“I’m not playing hard-to-get. I don’t think there’s anything you could say or do that would ever make me want to sleep with you. Hell, I’m certain more than half of Carolina Beach already has.”

His face falls for a second, but he recovers quickly. If I had to guess, he wasn't expecting this much resistance. Something tells me he's not used to being rejected.

"How the hell would you know?" he barks, the tension in his neck and shoulders growing stiff, his eyes narrowing into slits.

"This isn't the first time we've met." I smile, thoroughly enjoying this little taste of karma on my lips. I reach my hand out between us and say, "You may not recognize me, but my name is Ivy Thomas. I wish I could say it was nice to see you again, but we both know that's not true. Ain't that right, Brix?"

His eyes widen in recollection before a salacious grin spreads across his arrogant face.

"Ivy fuckin' Thomas. It's too fucking bad, even knowing that I'd still fuck you like it's the best you'll ever have."

"You're a real prick."

"So I've been told." Brix takes a swig of his beer, not taking his eyes off me.

"Yo, Brix!" a voice booms through the speaker. We both turn our attention toward the stage to find their other bandmate, Tysin, staring back at us with his hands up and an annoyed expression on his face.

"If you change your mind, come find me after the show."

He has the fucking nerve to wink at me before he turns, heading toward Tysin, Madden joining them as they start setting up the rest of their band equipment.

"What did he say to you?" Kyla asks, returning with a beer bottle in her hand.

"He didn't even recognize me," I snicker. "Tried hitting on me, probably assuming he could convince me to come home with him. I turned that shit down real quick."

"You're kidding," she snorts.

"Not in the least. You should've seen the look on his face when I introduced myself."

"Oh my God, I can't believe I missed it." She giggles, looking both amused and disappointed.

We slide into our booth, catching up. We spot a few people I remember from high school who stop by to chat with us before the show starts.

I've watched the guys play before, although it was years ago when they played on their makeshift stage in Madden's garage. Thankfully, their dad eventually said they had to find somewhere else to keep their equipment, which meant they started coming around less and less.

When they take the stage a little while later, I try to avoid showing any interest, but even I can't deny they're good. I'm thankful for the lights being turned down, so I'm able to hide in the darkness from the possibility of Brix spotting me.

The last thing I want is for him to see me watching him or give him the satisfaction of thinking I'm enjoying his performance. I've seen a lot of bands play while pursuing a career in music journalism. I'd never utter these words to anyone, but I'm surprised they haven't been scooped up by a major record label. They're talented.

Brix smiles flirtatiously at the crowd while he sings, leaning over the speaker, letting the women in the front touch him, thrusting toward their roaming hands.

Tysin plays the bass guitar next to Brix, nodding his head to the beat of the music. Madden's size alone makes him hard to miss sitting behind his drums.

I watch in awe for most of their set before I decide to cut out early and head to my new home. Exhaustion from packing up my car and making the drive back to CB weighed on me. A text from my mom came through around midnight as she was boarding her red-eye flight home. She left me with detailed instructions on where to find her hide-a-key and directions to the room I'd be staying in for the summer.

When she called me last week, I was in the heat of finals. My workload was piled high, and every available minute was spent with my head crammed in my books. When she broke the news she had gotten engaged, I couldn't believe my ears.

Honestly, I never thought I'd see the day she'd want to get remarried after her divorce from my father. I spent an hour on the phone listening to her gush over the man, Jasper, she recently met and how she'd been swept away in their whirlwind romance ever since.

I was shocked when she broke the news that not only had he asked her to marry him, but she had also recently decided to move in. It wasn't a big deal to me in the grand scheme of things. We had bounced around from place to place throughout my childhood, so it wasn't like I was coming home to a familiar house I had lived in all my life only to find out it was now gone.

It made the decision to come home for the summer all the more difficult, but in the end, I needed the help. I needed to find a job and save up money, so when I went back to school, I could put all focus on my degree.

I wanted to find a way to enjoy the next couple of months while I was here, but nothing could've prepared me for what happened next.

CHAPTER TWO

BRIX

I don't remember who brought me home, much less why I chose to crash on the couch, of all places. My back screams in agony from the pain and stiffness, moving to stretch, peeking one eye open.

The piercing ray of sunlight combined with the skull-splitting headache has me regretting the round of shots we had after wrapping up our show last night.

It wasn't the first time it happened, and it won't be the last.

I miscalculate the space between me and the edge of the couch when I roll on my side, sending me falling face-first onto the hardwood floor.

"God damn," I groan, bracing my hands beneath me, pushing myself up. Feeling weak, I reach for the edge of the oak coffee table to help me up.

Beer cans litter the surface, reminding me of the one too many drinks I put away when I got home.

"What the hell was I thinking?"

I wince hearing the sound of a throat clearing behind me. I expect it to be my father, which should have me regretting my choices from last night even more. Except that would mean I gave a shit, which I don't. I stopped worrying about what he thought of me a long time ago.

I rub the pads of my fingers over my eyes, delaying the inevitable moment when I glance up to find him staring bullets through me, adding yet another reason for being a disgrace of a son to the list.

"Are you waiting for me to answer that question?"

The soft voice from behind catches me off guard, sending my head jolting over my shoulder. The sharp movement causes a shooting pain to slice up the column of my neck. I roll my eyes shut, groaning in agony.

Her quiet chuckle follows. Whoever it is clearly relishes in my pain.

Pushing to sit on the edge of the couch, I fall back against the cushions, tilting my head in her direction. When I finally manage to open my eyes enough, I wonder for a second if I somehow misplaced where I was or what the hell happened last night.

What was I thinking?

Did Ivy end up coming home with me?

Hell no.

Thinking back to the scant denim shorts she wore showing off her sculpted legs nearly has me biting my lip at all the thoughts swirling through my mind. My eyes rake over her body once again, pausing as they land on her tan legs.

She's active, judging by the clothes she's wearing combined with her tight body.

Recalling how she all too joyously turned me down, followed by the smirk lining those sexy-ass lips when she pointed out who she is, left the sting of embarrassment ringing clear in my memory.

Yeah... there's no way she would've come home with me. If that's the case, what the hell is she doing standing in my living room with the look of disdain painted like a neon sign on her face?

"What the hell are you doing here? Did you break into my fucking house? Or is this your way of twisting the knife deeper after last night?"

She laughs. The sound coming out both sexy and frustrating. Her head is thrown back and strands of her long, dark hair are falling over her shoulder.

"The fact you think I give a shit about you or would even consider wasting another second on your bullshit is hilarious."

Well, okay then. It still doesn't answer the question of why the hell she is in my house?

As if reading my mind, she continues, "I'm actually wondering the same thing." She clenches her jaw. She looks so fucking sexy, the way her cheeks turn rosy. If this is how she looks when she's mad, I can't wait to see her when she's turned on.

"Like I said, sweetheart"—I lean forward, bracing my hands on my knees to stand— "this is my house. I live here."

Facing her now, the subtle tick in her jaw at the term of endearment does not escape me. Anger blazes in her eyes when she crosses her arms in front of her chest. She widens her stance like she's gearing up for the argument that's about to ensue.

"Are you sure you still don't want to take me up on my offer from last night? I have no problem letting you take a little aggression out on me."

I reach my hand out, brushing my knuckle along the ink covering her forearm. Goose bumps rise over her skin, and despite her best effort to paste the look of hatred on her face, her body gives her away. She's trying to play it off, hoping like hell I won't notice, but I flash her a grin letting her know she's not fooling me.

"Something tells me the hate-sex will be some of the best fucking I've ever had," I moan, wrapping my hand around her wrist.

She grits her teeth, whipping her arm out of my hold. Seeing how riled up she is, I bite my lip to cover my bemused smile. I have a feeling I'm going to enjoy letting her take her anger out on me.

Nails in my back, teeth marking my skin. *Fuck.*

"If you think I'd ever let your dick anywhere near me, you've gotta be fuckin' crazy. I bet you have shit growing on you from all the places that thing's been."

"You better watch your fuckin' mouth," I grunt, tension coiling in my body, taking a step closer to her. She smiles like the Cheshire cat, apparently liking how she's pissed me off.

Yeah, the hate-sex is gonna be real fuckin' good for the both of us.

A familiar sound of keys sliding into the lock followed by the click of the deadbolt has us both turning toward the door. Laughter filters through the room, and my eyes bounce back over to Ivy. The smell of her clean scent washes over me; the way her throat bobs when she swallows ignites a fire within me.

"Mother?" Ivy says, sounding both surprised and lighter. Like happiness was wrapped around one simple word. That is until I realize it's my father and his fiancée, Charlene, staring back at us.

For a second, I wonder if they heard us arguing from outside.

"Ivyana," she replies, smiling, and it all clicks into place.

My mind filters through the several conversations we've had about her daughter, Ivyana. The daughter who graduated high school with honors and has a nearly perfect GPA at the University of North Carolina.

Ivy is Ivyana. What the hell is wrong with me? Why didn't it click into place until now? I've never heard her called by her full name, not even when we were back in high school.

"Hi, Mother." She grins, crossing the distance between them to wrap her in a hug. The snarky tone she threw at me a moment ago is completely gone, replaced with something else entirely.

Reaching my hand up behind my neck, I massage my fingers into my skin in hopes of easing the tension.

"I'm so happy to see you, honey. I've missed you."

Already over this bullshit, I begin picking up the beer cans strewn over the coffee table along with the ones knocked over onto the floor.

"Brix, what the hell happened here?"

It wouldn't be a typical day if my father wasn't finding some reason to lay into me.

"What's it look like? I had a few drinks last night after my show. I'll fuckin' clean it up, alright? Chill out."

Holding the cans in my palm, I brush past my father, stalking into the kitchen. Like whiplash, the once happy moment between Ivy and her mom is gone.

"This can't happen anymore. You hear me? Just because I let you live here doesn't mean you can treat my place like a dumpster."

"Yeah, I got it."

"I'm serious, Brix," he demands, raising his voice even louder, "turn around and look at me."

Tossing the cans into the recycle bin, I turn the faucet on and wash my hands before grabbing the towel. Resting my hip on the edge of the counter, I stare at him with a look I hope says *get on with it already*.

"This cannot happen anymore."

"I heard you the first time. I said I got it."

Charlene whispers something to him about waiting until later to have this talk. He nods, apparently ready to let it go.

We only agreed I'd stay here because I promised to help look after the place. His job has him traveling a lot. Even when he's in town between trips, he usually stayed at the apartment near his office. It got to the point he was either going to sell the house or hire a groundskeeper.

"I'm glad to see you've met Ivyana. She's Charlene's daughter. You may remember us discussing her staying here for the summer. I didn't want the two of you to meet this way." He glances at Ivy, and she flashes him a warm smile as he says, "It's good to see you again."

Again? I thought.

"I didn't want you to meet this way," he repeats, "or for you two to find out under these circumstances." His eyes bounce back over to Charlene. She steps closer to him, grabbing his hand.

Ivy's eyes widen in bewilderment as if hanging on his every word waiting for what bomb he's about to drop. I know what's about to come before the words are even out of his mouth.

"Charlene and I... while we were away on vacation, we decided to get married."

"What the—?" I stammer.

At the same moment, Ivy says, "Oh my God!"

"Are you serious?" I scoff.

My father's eyes lock on mine, and I can see the daggers he's shooting my way the moment they do.

If he thinks I'm going to stay here and play house with them, he's out of his damn mind.

"Now you listen here, I won't tolerate any of your comments. If you have something to say, I suggest you swallow it. I don't have the time or patience to hear you anymore."

Tossing the towel in my hand to the counter, I cross my arms over my chest.

Ignoring my father's glare, I focus on Ivy. Her hand covers her mouth, and a dazed look shrouds her eyes when she peers over at me.

What the fuck?

If they are married, this makes Ivy, or should I say Ivyana, my sister. Judging by the wide-eyed look on her face, it's apparent the same thought just hit her, too.

I told my stepsister I wanted to fuck all my frustration out on her. Good fucking lord.

"I can't believe it, Mom," Ivy says, hugging her once again. Charlene holds her hand out between the two of them to show her the ring. Of course, like every one of my father's wives, they can't help but gush over their five-carat diamond ring.

"Wow, Mom," she says in awe, reaching for her hand, "it's beautiful."

"Well, let's hope you signed a prenup with this one. Huh, Dad?" I snicker, crossing through the kitchen toward the staircase leading to my bedroom.

"Brix Carter Ward, don't fucking move."

I stop momentarily, waiting for whatever insults he wants to hurl my way. Although, he's always been one to say them without other watchful eyes around us, so I know the real jabs will come later when it's just the two of us.

"I won't tolerate you talking bad about Charlene or our marriage. If you have a problem, I suggest you find a way to keep your mouth shut, or you can get the hell out of here."

"You got it," I mutter, deadpan.

"By that, I mean you aren't allowed at the beach house either. If you're out of here, you're on your own."

"Whatever. Congratulations, Charlene. You picked a real winner."

Not bothering to look her in the eyes as I say it, I stalk up the stairs toward my room.

Passing by the bathroom, I find the guest room door next to mine open. Pausing in the doorway, I notice the bed sitting directly across from me left unmade and two suitcases standing near the foot of the bed.

It looks like Ivy's made herself at home in her new house, in the bedroom next to mine. I can tell already it's gonna be a long fuckin' summer.

CHAPTER THREE

IVY

Standing with my jaw half hung open, I'm stunned. Not only did my mom drop the bomb she's married, but Brix, the same prick from my high school years, is now my step-brother.

Until two weeks ago, I didn't think I'd see the day my mother would ever dream of getting married again. She had always remained adamant marriage wasn't for her. She hadn't even dated anyone seriously, at least not to my knowledge, for the topic to even come up.

"Mom, I just...I'm... wow! I can't believe it," I mutter, eyes wide. Shaking myself from my thoughts, I hold her hand, staring down at the beautiful rock on her finger. It's stunning, huge, and honestly looks so out of place sitting perfectly on her finger.

"Congratulations."

What doesn't look out of place is the beaming smile on her face. The joy she's radiating is a glow I haven't seen her wear in a very long time. Immediately, I want to say something to smooth over the bitter comments Brix just spewed.

His father may have other ex-wives or reasons for believing a prenup is necessary, but I know without a doubt, my mom wouldn't care either way. She's not a money-hungry, materialistic woman. Whatever he thinks could happen between them, he's wrong about her.

"I'm so happy for you." I smile, and I mean it genuinely.

"Thank you, honey. It means a lot to me to hear this coming from you. I'm so glad to have you home."

"Thanks, Mom." She flashes me a warm smile, tears filling her beautiful green eyes. I hate seeing her cry, so I pull her into another hug.

"If you don't mind, I'm going to go freshen up. Our flight was early, and I want to get out of these clothes."

"Yeah, of course." I step back when she leans down to adjust her carry-on over her shoulder, reaching for the handle on her luggage.

"I need to get everything situated, too. I'm in the room down the hall on the left. I hope that's the right one?"

"Absolutely," Jasper states. "Make yourself at home. Please ignore my son, too. He's mouthy and inconsiderate sometimes, but I believe the man I raised him to be is still in there somewhere."

Jasper reaches his hand out, stopping my mother's steps. He takes her luggage and she leans in to kiss him on his cheek, smiling as she walks across the living room toward their bedroom.

Picking up my tennis shoes I dropped in the entryway last night, I quickly tie them on my feet, grab my water, and head out the front door.

Originally, I planned to get in a quick run, but with so many thoughts swirling around my head, I decide against it. Sticking my earbuds in, I click the call button on my phone.

"Hey," Kyla's heavy sigh greets me, followed by a light, rustling sound.

"Hey, sorry. I didn't mean to wake you up."

"It's all good. I need to get my ass out of bed anyway. What's up? You sound serious..." She pauses. "Is everything alright?"

"Not at all." I run my hand over the top of my hair, wrapping the strands of my ponytail around my fist.

"Uh, oh. What happened?"

"You know how I told you my mom got engaged? It turns out they went and got married. You'll never guess to who."

"WHO?" Her voice raises like three octaves, causing me to hold the phone away from my face, wincing.

"Jasper Ward. Brix's dad."

For a second, I think the line disconnects when she goes completely silent.

"You there?"

"No fuckin' way!"

"Yeah..." I trail off.

When I reach the end of the street, I make a left turn, heading down the long hill leading through the neighborhood. I take in the sight of the sun rising in the distance, the quiet sounds of nature waking up around me. If my mind wasn't carried away in the shitstorm I left behind me, I would've stopped to admire its beauty.

"Why do I feel like there is more to this story?"

"Well, I woke up to find Brix half-naked, hungover, and passed out on the couch."

She laughs. "Sounds about right."

"He had the nerve to bring up last night. We got into a heated argument, and the asshole had the gall to say something about how the hate-sex was going to be the best he's ever had or some bullshit."

My mind drifts off remembering the look on his face when he said it. Brix is sexy in a rugged sort of way. He knows it, too, and he uses his good looks and charm to get whatever he wants. He's the type of guy your parents warn you to stay away from, but the one all the girls wish they could claim.

Brix isn't the type of guy you want to be mixed up with. He's a notorious player. He may have a reputation for being excellent in bed, but he'll wreak havoc on your heart.

Not to mention, he's now my stepbrother.

"Why does it sound like you're wondering if he's right?"

"Excuse me?" My voice is now high-pitched, calling me out on my own bluff.

Alright, so the thought crossed my mind. Sue me.

Kyla's obnoxious laughter barks through the phone, and I regret even telling her about it in the first place.

"I thought you were supposed to listen to me vent. You're not helping right now."

"Helping with what? You're the one thinking about what it'd be like to screw Brix."

"Still not helping."

"Alright, alright," she sighs. "I'm sorry. Seriously, could you imagine if last night had gone differently and you had gone home with him? How traumatized you would've been waking up and doing the walk of shame as your mom walked through the front door?"

"Oh. My. God. We're not friends anymore. This conversation is over."

"Okay, sorry. I'm done."

"Thank you."

"For today."

"Kyla," I chide, "I'm about to hang up on you."

"Alright, fine. I'll stop. At least tell me what happened."

I spend the next twenty minutes walking through the streets of my new neighborhood venting about how terrible my morning was. Growing up, we mostly lived in apartments. It was only my mom and me, so it wasn't like we needed a ton of space.

Looking at some of these houses, their perfectly manicured lawns, and their white picket fences, I feel oddly out of place. This wasn't, and never has been, our world. As much as I hate the idea of living in the same house with Brix, the thought of taking a dip in their massive pool I spotted outside does sound relaxing.

"I have to figure out what I'm going to do for a job while I'm back. I need to save up money, which will also get me out of the house. Got any ideas?"

"Why don't you apply at Whiskey Barrel?"

Thinking back to the bar we met up at last night, I consider her suggestion. It was packed for most of the night. I can only imagine the tips the bartenders rake in on a Friday night alone.

"I'll consider it. I need to figure something out soon, though."

We make plans to meet up for lunch early next week as I finish up the rest of my walk. Just as I'm turning to head back up the driveway toward the house, I've decided I'll turn in an application at Whiskey Barrel.

While it may not be the best idea, considering it's Brix's stomping ground, I need a job, and in a couple months, I'll be hitting the pavement out of here anyway.

When I make it back to the house, I quickly grab my stuff from my suitcase, not bothering to waste my time unpacking yet. I jump in the shower to clean up before heading over to the bar.

Before I take off, I glance over the balcony down into the living room, and there's no sign of my mom or Jasper. Just as the thought creeps into my mind, music begins blaring from the room at the end of the hallway. By the sound of the bass reverberating through the floor, I'm going to make a wild guess it's coming from Brix's room.

The door is open, just barely, and against my better judgment, I take the two steps toward the door, wondering what he's doing.

Bracing my hand against the edge of the door frame, I hold my breath while peering through the crack.

"Can I help you?" The sound of his voice coming from behind me sends my back collapsing against the wall, holding a hand over my chest.

"What the hell, Brix? You scared the shit out of me."

"My bad. It's my fault I snuck up behind you like I did," he deadpans, not sounding the least bit apologetic.

I roll my eyes, knowing he's caught me.

Unlike earlier when he woke up, he's now dressed in a pair of distressed jeans and a cut-off muscle shirt with a "rock on" fist printed on the front. His hair looks wild like he ran his hand through the strands at least a dozen times.

"So, this is what it's like having a nosey sister. Does this mean I get to sneak into your room when you're not home and go through your shit?"

"You wouldn't." My jaw flexes.

If I find out he's messed with my stuff, he's going to have a lot more to deal with than me peeking through his door.

He takes a step toward me, crowding my space. My chest heaves with every strangled breath I take. His eyes roam over my face, dropping to my chest as he leans in. With my head pressed firmly against the wall, I have nowhere to go. He has me trapped, right where he wants me.

"What? Would you prefer I snuck into your room when you *were* home?"

My tongue darts out, licking my dry lips, trying to form a response. I watch in rapt attention when his eyes fall to my lips, his jaw clenching and nostrils flaring.

"What would you prefer, Ivy? Are you thinking about me sneaking into your room, crawling into your bed next to you when you're asleep at night?"

"What?" My eyes widen in shock. He can't be serious.

"Tell me you're not picturing it now. Fuck, I'm gonna be hard as a rock lying in my bed tonight, thinking about you in the room next to mine waiting for me."

"You're out of your mind."

"Am I?" he asks, leaning in closer, "What will you be wearing for me?"

I press my hands against his chest, pushing him away. He stumbles, falling back against the wall on the opposite side of the hall.

"If you come in my room, the only thing waiting for you will be a swift kick in the balls."

Turning on my heel, I storm off, leaving him bent over at the waist, laughing behind me. I don't have time for his bullshit.

CHAPTER FOUR

IVY

I ended up stopping into the Whiskey Barrel later that day. Turns out the owner, Jayde, was in a desperate need for help, which worked out for me since it meant she had me starting the following weekend with a full schedule ahead. Tonight was my first night, and I couldn't stop the nervous jitters when I showed up.

"Here, we'll have you wear this." Jayde tosses me a black shirt to wear. She catches me off guard, reaching one hand out to grab it before it hits the floor.

"Works for me." I hold the Whiskey Barrel t-shirt in front of me, checking the size.

"I'll have a couple tank tops for you in a day or so. I'm waiting for the shipment to get in."

I slip the shirt over my head, tying the cotton material at my waist and cuffing the sleeves. Jayde smiles warmly at me before turning to head back to the front of the bar.

A cute blonde turns the corner, stopping in front of the time clock, grabs a card, and swipes it through the reader before sliding it back into the rack on the wall.

"Hey!" She smiles. "You must be the new girl."

I recognize her from the night I was here with Kyla, as she slips her phone in her back pocket. Her makeup is done and her hair curls in waves over her shoulder. She's beautiful, and I'm willing to bet she makes a killing on busy nights.

"That would be me. I'm Ivy." I reach out, shaking her hand.

"Oaklyn."

"Nice to meet you."

"Back at ya. You ready for tonight? It's going to be a busy onc."

"Bring it on. I desperately need the money."

"A Rebels Havoc always brings in a crowd, so be ready."

I hadn't even realized they'd be playing again tonight. Brix and I have managed to stay clear of each other the past few days. It's one thing to be surprised and find out your mom went off and got married. It's something else entirely when you realize your new stepbrother is the same jackass who used to get off on making your life a living hell growing up.

It's for the best if we avoid each other for the rest of the summer. Although it'll be hard to do with him sleeping in the room right next door to mine, I've gotta try.

The night kicks off, and Oaklyn is right; it's busy. It's shortly after eight o'clock when the bouncer near the door mentions we've hit capacity. A Rebels Havoc isn't even set to take the stage until nine.

I'm able to sneak away for a quick minute to run to the bathroom. I swiftly wash my hands before I slip out the door, past a crowd of people leading back out to the dance floor. There's a swarm of people standing near the stage, waiting for the band to start. I hear him before I see him, his mouth pressed against my ear. Glancing down, I see the ink covering the top of his arm banded around my waist, holding me against his front.

"Don't you think you should fix your shirt? You're a little underdressed."

"Excuse me," I bite back, pushing his hand away, turning to face him.

"I said, fix your shirt. No one wants to see that." He reaches for the toothpick sticking out of his mouth, gesturing toward me like the way my shirt is knotted is the most outrageous thing he's ever seen.

"Well, that's funny. Wasn't it just a few days ago you were saying how you were picturing sneaking into my room to have, what was it you called it, hate-sex with me?" I hold my hands up using air quotes.

He scoffs, looking at something over my shoulder before his eyes find mine once again. I swear to God, I want to smack the smug look off his face. The only reason why he's even treating me like this is because he's mad that I rejected him. Twice.

"Rejection isn't a good look on you."

His eyes narrow, clenching his jaw. He knows I've called him out.

"Nah, Poison Ivy. I hated you then just like I hate you now."

The mention of the name he used to throw at me still stings like it did all those years ago. He was the instigator of all the bullshit I went through. The mere mention of the name makes my blood boil.

He's full of shit, and we both know it. If he thinks I'm the same scared girl who's going to cower in the corner, he has another thing coming.

Pressing my palm against his chest, I step in closer to him, removing all distance between us until we're standing toe-to-toe. Wrapping my hand around his neck, I pull him until our foreheads are nearly touching.

The move takes him off guard. The subtle scent of his cologne hits me, and for a second, I wish he was anyone else other than who he is to me. I swear I can feel his heart hammering against my hand, his breath feathering across my lips. His eyes narrow, falling on my mouth. I wonder if he's thinking the same thing I am, before meeting my eyes once again.

Lifting my leg, I carefully brush my knee over the front of his pants. If I didn't know better, I'd swear I could feel his hard dick straining against his zipper. His jaw ticks from the movement when I quirk my eyebrow up at him, a smirk lining my mouth.

He knows I've caught him.

"I think your body gave you away."

Running my hand down his chest further, I stop when I reach his waistband. His eyes drop to my hand, waiting for my next move, when I step back, releasing my hold on him.

"Like I said, Brix, rejection isn't a good look on you. That's the closest I'll ever get to your disease-infected dick. No worries though, by the looks of this crowd, you'll have no problem finding a place to get it wet."

The arrogant grin returns. He slips the toothpick back in his mouth. Not bothering to waste another second of energy on him, I shoulder past him through the crowd back toward the bar.

I feel terrible for getting caught up with Brix. I left them hanging longer than I intended. Judging by the line forming, they're in desperate need of my help.

Stepping behind the bar, his voice filters through the speakers surrounding us.

"Well, hello there." His voice is deep like it's dipped in sex.

The women in the crowd cheer and I can picture the arrogant smile on his face without even bothering to look up at him.

"Fuck yeah." He laughs. I give in and glance over. Even from here, I know he's staring right at me. "I'm lookin' to bring one of you home with me and want you yelling just like that, all night long."

He punctuates each word with his hips thrusting toward the crowd.

"Where were you?" Jayde asks, coming up behind me to grab a bottle of vodka.

"Sorry, I had to run to the bathroom. The line was long."

She hesitates for a second, flipping the bottle to fill the shot glass in front of her. For a moment, I worry I'm busted for lying, wondering if maybe she caught me talking to Brix.

I reach into the cooler, grabbing a bottle of beer before popping the top and sliding it across the bar, swiping the cash off the counter to ring up the order.

Jayde doesn't respond, turning to head back into the cooler to refill the ice. I'm relieved. I need this job; the last thing I want is to burn a bridge on my first night.

Madden starts on the drums as Tysin joins in before Brix starts to sing. I recognize the song from the first night I was here. It isn't hard to get lost in the sound of the music.

The last time I watched them play, I had been so distracted watching Brix, I hadn't paid much attention to Tysin and Madden. Growing up, Kyla was always dragging me out to the garage to watch them play. She'd deny it if Madden ever found out, but I knew even back then it was more about being around Tysin than anything.

He was the sole reason she wanted us to come out last weekend. Not that Madden would ever let anything happen between them, but it didn't stop her from hoping.

Tysin is dressed in a t-shirt that says, "You're killin' me Smalls" with a giant picture of Biggie Smalls on the front. He has gauges in his ears and a chain hanging from his jeans. His hair is covered by the backward hat.

Madden, on the other hand, is disguised behind his drum set wearing a hat, along with a pair of shades covering his eyes.

I did my best to keep my focus on tending bar, but it was difficult with the way Brix talked to the crowd in between songs. At one point, he took his shirt off. Watching women grab at him, nearly pulling his pants down, had me wincing, and I wasn't sure why.

He really didn't have an ounce of dignity.

"Don't worry, you'll get used to it. He's always like that," Oaklyn snickers, shaking her head.

It takes me a second to piece together who she's talking about until she nods her head toward the stage.

"Brix."

"What about him?"

"The look of disgust is written all over your face, girl." She laughs. "He's always like this when they play. He loves feeding off the women in the crowd. He's quite the attention whore."

"Oh, trust me, I know! We grew up together. I'm just amazed women actually find this attractive."

Oaklyn giggles awkwardly but in a way that says she's guilty and I've called her out.

"I'm sorry. I didn't mean, I'm sorry...I didn't mean to offend you."

She waves me off. "He has many layers to him and can be really sweet when he wants to be. We've never hooked up or anything. I've been here when he's come in to drown his sorrows a time or two, though."

The thought of Oaklyn and Brix together has me looking around the bar, wondering who has been with him. Why do I even care who he's slept with?

Maybe because he's tried to sleep with me, too? Or maybe it's because I've felt the pull toward him and I've actually given it thought?

The images die, though, the moment I start thinking of how he spoke to me in the hallway earlier. Oaklyn said he has many layers, more like multiple personalities. He's always been hot and cold with me, going from one side to the other.

If he thinks he can get to me this summer, he's dead wrong.

CHAPTER FIVE

BRIX

"Thanks for comin' out tonight. We're A Rebels Havoc, we hope you enjoyed the show."

Pressing my foot against the speaker, I lean over into the crowd touching the hands of those in the front row.

"If you're single, stick around. We don't have to let the good time end here."

Standing back, my eyes search the crowd as cheers ring out.

Despite her blatant hatred for me, I've caught Ivy watching us a few times while she's been bartending. She may play it off like she hates me, but I saw the way her body reacted to my touch. The subtle tremble that raked through her, how her hands grabbed onto my forearm, holding onto me and not at all pushing me away. Not at first anyway.

Stepping off the stage and into the dressing room, I grab my handkerchief from my back pocket and wipe the sweat dripping from my brow. It was a packed crowd tonight and a ton of fun. Whiskey Barrel is one of my favorite places in town to play for this very reason.

"She really has you in knots, doesn't she?" Tysin jokes. It takes me a second to realize he's talking to me.

"'Scuse me?"

"You heard me. That last comment at the end about being single. It got anything to do with Ivy rejecting you and talking shit about your diseased dick?" Tysin chuckles, his grin nearly taking over his face. He holds a fist in front of his mouth, attempting to contain his laughter.

"I don't give two shits about what she has to say."

"Is that right?"

"Yeah. Why don't you worry about your own dick?"

"I think you care a lot more than you want to let on."

"What makes you fucking think that?" I ask, picking up my hat from the table in the back where we left our stuff sitting. Pulling it over my head, I lean against the edge of the table and cross my arms. Tysin is always quick to run his mouth, and I'm sick of his bullshit.

"The first night she was here with Kyla, you were all up on her, hoping she'd come home with you. The second you found out who she was, and she rejected your ass, you were back to being the same piece of shit you were to her years ago."

My eyes narrow, knowing he's only doing this to get a rise out of me. I'm not going to give him the satisfaction.

"I could have her ass eating out of the palm of my hand if I wanted to. I'm not fucking interested in her. I didn't recognize her from all those years ago, but it doesn't matter. Now, I just like getting a rise out of her."

"Mmmhm."

I clench my jaw, taking the three steps separating us. We stand toe-to-toe. Tysin's mouth curves up on the edges, loving how he's getting under my skin.

"I bet by the end of the summer, not only will I fuck her, but I'll send her heartbroken ass back to wherever the fuck she came from."

"You want me to bet you you'll fuck your stepsister?"

"You heard me."

"You really are the asshole she thinks you are."

"I'll tell you the same thing I told her, I hated her then, and I hate her now. I don't give a shit what she thinks of me. Hell, I don't give a fuck what you think, either."

"Well, this oughta be interesting."

Tysin grabs the can of beer from the ice bucket left on the table, pops the tab, and takes a long pull. He tips his beer toward me before he ducks out of the room and into the packed bar.

"You don't really mean that, do you?" Madden asks from behind me.

"Stay out of it, Madd," I reply sternly, brushing him off.

"No, dude. You can't tell me you're actually going to go through with this shit, are you?"

He looks at me, trying to read my emotions, and I hate how he can always see through me.

"Man, you really can be a prick sometimes. Ya know that?"

"I hadn't heard that before." I roll my eyes. "What's it to you anyway? Am I stomping on your pussy grounds?"

He barks out a laugh, shaking his head. "Nah, man. She grew up with Kyla, they're like sisters, but it's not what you think. Just let it go, will ya?"

"I need a beer," I say, grabbing one from the bucket before I shoulder past him and head to join the rest of the bar.

For the rest of the night, I do my best to stay clear of Ivy. Oaklyn stops by our table, refilling our bucket with beer. They've already decided they're going to call an Uber for a ride. I'm not about to leave my truck in the parking lot overnight, so I only have a couple beers throughout the night, wanting to be okay to drive home.

The bar is nearly empty when I head out. The sun has long since gone down, and a storm has started to roll in. Raindrops beat down on the cement as I make the jog across the lot toward my pickup.

I fully planned to bring home a chick with me. In fact, there was this sweet-as-sin blonde I'd been eyeing most of the night. She was wearing a sexy dress with fuck-me heels. Despite picturing those heels digging into my back, I said fuck it and left. After my conversation with Tysin and Madden, I was in a piss-poor mood and ready to go home.

Climbing into my pickup, I lift my shirt to wipe the rain from my face before I make the short drive. I'm turning onto Franklin Street, only a couple miles from my house, when I see a car pulled over on the shoulder with their caution lights on.

It's difficult to make out the car with the rain falling hard against my windshield. I don't think anything of it until I get closer and notice the rust bucket parked on the side of the road looks exactly like Ivy's. As soon as I pass her, I pull over on the shoulder and put my truck in park.

I hold my hand up, shielding my face from the rain when I hop out. There's a strange smell coming from her car, mixed with the scent of moisture in the air. Right away, I know she has some sort of leak. It can't be good for her to drive, even if it's only a short distance away. Not to mention, it's late and not safe for her to be walking alone, on top of the cold and the rain.

Approaching the driver's side, Ivy's form is barely visible beneath the rain beating against the car.

Pounding my hand on the window, I shout through the glass, "You alright? You want a ride?"

"What the hell are you doing here?"

"I saw you pulled over on the side of the road. What the hell does it look like I'm doing?"

The rain picks up, hammering down on me, soaking my hair and shirt in the process.

"Do you want a ride or not?" I shout.

"No, it's fine. I've got a way."

"What's that exactly? You gonna walk home in this by yourself?" I ask, holding my arms out around me.

"I'm not an idiot, Brix. I know more about cars than you think I do. I'll figure it out for myself."

I'm standing here outside her car with the storm rolling in overhead and she still wants to sit here and argue with me. I swear, she's the most infuriating woman I've ever met.

Holding my hands up in surrender, I take a step back. "Fine. More power to ya."

I turn to head back to my truck when she rolls down the window and hollers, "Wait!"

Glancing over my shoulder at her, I see the struggle on her face, not wanting to ask me for help. "Can you give me a ride home?"

There's a veil of exhaustion in her eyes. She rubs her hands over her face, brushing the wet strands of hair out of the way.

"Yeah, let's go."

She slides the window back up and jumps out. Clutching her purse against her chest, she slams the door and uses the remote to lock it. We both hold our hands up to shield our faces, making the run toward my pickup.

Ivy climbs into the passenger side next to me, shutting the door behind us. The sound of the radio playing low, mixed with the soft raindrops on the truck fills the silence around us. The energy in the cab of the truck has changed, and all I can think about is the smell of her flowery perfume.

Her fingers twist in her lap in front of her. The soft glow of the dashboard illuminates the cab just enough to see her face. We're both soaking wet. Ivy's lip trembles and goose bumps break out on her skin. Pulling my t-shirt over my head, I toss it on the floor between us while turning the heat on high. She mutters a low "thank you."

"If you're cold, you can always slide over here. I can keep you warm."

Her eyes dart over to mine, narrowing. "Oh, you're back to this now. Wasn't it a few hours ago you were acting like you were disgusted looking at me?"

Her throat bobs when she says it, making me realize it bothers her a whole lot more than she's letting on.

"You should know better by now than to take anything I say personally. I'm a shit liar, Ivy."

I'm not sure what I expected her to say or do next, but she takes me off guard completely when she pulls her t-shirt over her head and tosses it on the floor with mine. She's left dressed only in a black lace bra, drawing my attention away from her eyes down to her breasts, traveling further to the soft curves of her hips.

"Yeah, you are," she says matter-of-factly, eyes blazing into me as mine eat up every inch of her body.

I shake myself from my thoughts, focusing on putting the truck in drive. I signal and pull onto the road. The sooner I can get us both home, the quicker we can put some much-needed distance between us.

"You guys played well tonight."

Her compliment takes me by surprise. I hadn't expected her to say it, especially after I'd been such an asshole to her earlier.

"Thanks. I caught you watching us a couple of times. I'm glad you liked it."

She smiles briefly, before biting her lip to cover it up. I don't even think through my next words before they're out of my mouth.

"If you want, I can take a look at your car for you tomorrow. See what's going on before you drag it into the shop."

My dad mentioned the reason why she was back home was to save up some money before her next semester. Hell, I'm pretty sure tonight was her first shift at Whiskey Barrel. I doubt she wanted to throw any extra cash at her piece of shit car.

"It's okay. You don't have to worry about it. I'll figure it out tomorrow."

"Alright, well, if you end up needing a ride anywhere, you know where to find me."

Pulling into the driveway, the house is dark, and the storm shows no signs of letting up any time soon as lightning cracks overhead, and the rumbles of thunder are felt rolling through.

Ivy peers out through the windshield, her arms still shivering as droplets of water drip from her hair onto her arms.

She glances over to me, her eyes locking on mine. The urge to reach out and touch her consumes me. If I didn't know better, I'd say she wants me to, too.

"Thanks for the ride, Brix."

She gives me a half-ass smile, leaning forward to pick up her purse and t-shirt, clutching them both against her chest. She reaches for the door handle, hesitating for a second. Letting out a heavy sigh, she pushes it open and quickly jumps out. Slamming it behind her, she makes a mad dash toward the door, disappearing from my sight through the heavy rain, leaving me alone with nothing but the smell of her still wrapped around me.

Fuck.

CHAPTER SIX

IVY

Shortly after I woke up and got out of the shower the next morning, I got a call which caught me completely off guard. The local auto shop, Miller's Auto, was letting me know my car was ready for pick up.

Immediately, I thought it had been ticketed and towed in, but when he told me the cost of the repairs, I knew that couldn't have been the case. The police don't look for stranded, broken down vehicles on the side of the road in desperate need of saving.

"I'm sorry, what? My car was towed to you?"

The man on the other end of the line pauses, seemingly confused by my question.

"Yes..." His voice trails off.

"I'm sorry, I just hadn't expected it. Can you tell me who had it towed?"

The sound of papers shuffling filter through the other end of the phone.

"Oh," he says, surprised. "It was Brix. The name on the credit card bill is for Brix Ward," he responds gruffly.

"Wait, what? You mean Brix paid the bill?"

There is another long pause before he replies, "Yes, ma'am. That's what it looks like."

I guess I shouldn't be too shocked. The only person who even knew was Brix, but after the way he talked to me at the bar, I hadn't expected him to give me a ride, let alone have my car towed to the auto shop to be fixed.

"Okay..." I pause. "I'll be by to pick it up shortly. Thank you."

Hitting the end button, I drop my phone in my lap from where I sit at the end of my bed gazing out the window overlooking the backyard. The sun has begun to rise in the distance. It had stormed long into the night. I've learned Brix likes to fall asleep to the sound of music playing, but I was thankful last night he didn't bother. I opened the window letting the sound of raindrops pounding on the ground outside lull me to sleep. It was the first good night's sleep I've had since moving here.

In the distance, I hear the bathroom door creak open and feet padding on the carpeted floor. A second later, he's standing in front of me, peeking through the crack in the door and our eyes connect. Pushing on the wood, he sends it swinging open and my eyes fall to his bare chest to the black boxer briefs fitting oh-so snuggly around his, ahem, package.

Good fucking lord. This man is so beyond sexy, it's downright sinful.

I can't help myself. My eyes scan over his body, mentally documenting every inch into my mind for permanent reference. The longer I stare at him, the more I start to question myself on why I decided it was a bad idea to hook up with him.

Oh, because he's my stepbrother. Right!

He leans his shoulder against the doorway, the movement snapping me out of my daze. I shake myself from my thoughts, remembering the conversation I had on the phone a moment ago.

There's a crooked grin lining his mouth, and I can't help my eye roll knowing how much he's enjoying being on the receiving end of my blatant perusal.

"Why didn't you tell me you had my car towed?"

"I had your car towed."

I bite down on my lower lip, fighting off the urge to smile.

"You didn't have to, ya know."

"Yep."

"So, why did you?"

"Would you rather I left your broken-down rust bucket on the side of the road?"

"I just mean I could've handled it."

"It's called a favor. Most people say, 'thank you' and move on."

"Thank you."

He doesn't reply, simply nods his head. Tightening his fist around the towel rolled up in his hand, he presses off the door frame and backs up.

"Um... could you possibly give me a ride over to pick it up? Jayde texted me to say I forgot to collect my tips from last night. I'm not sure what I owe you, but I'll give you what I have and, if it's cool with you, I'll pay you the rest with my next paycheck. Hopefully, I'll earn enough over the weekend."

"I'm not worried about it. Give me a few to shower and, uh, get decent. We can head over after."

Nodding my head, my eyes drop down to his waistband again when he turns. The visible bulge barely contained by the cotton stretched across his waist has me struggling to swallow.

Brix chuckles, muttering something under his breath. I can't be entirely sure, but it sounded like he said, "Be careful."

A few moments later, I hear the door click shut and the sound of water running in the bathroom next to my room.

I squeeze my eyes tight as mental images from last night flit through my mind. How he looked standing outside my car in the rain, to the way his hips gyrated in front of the crowd. I imagine him standing naked in the shower, looking all too delicious like he had a moment ago, and it makes my mouth water.

I force myself to my feet and focus on finding something to wear and fixing my hair before we pick up my car. It's nearly twenty minutes later when my hair is dry and my clothes are on when I realize the sound of the water next door is still on.

What the hell is taking him so long? I still need to do my makeup and style my hair, and everything I need is left in the bathroom with him.

Standing outside the bathroom door, I hesitate for a second before I knock lightly and check the knob to see if it's locked.

"Yeah!" His voice shouts.

Opening the door slightly, I peek my head in enough to ask, "Are you almost done? Or can I grab my stuff out of the cabinet quick?"

"Go for it."

His response causes my adrenaline to spike, opening the door enough to slip inside. Steam billows around me from the intense heat. I take a deep breath, pushing myself to grab what I need and get out.

Swiping my brush from the drawer near the sink, I let my eyes chance a glance at the mirror and my lungs seize in my chest with the sudden inhale of breath. Even through the sheen of fog covering the glass, I can still make out Brix's form through the opaque shower curtain.

I track his movements, the way his muscular arm runs over his chest and his head tilts back under the water until my eyes fall to his jerking movements down below.

My eyes widen in shock, and I'm frozen in place. I struggle to keep hold of the brush in my hand, sending it crashing into the sink, watching his hand wrapped around his length as his hips thrust forward. I don't want to blink, afraid if I move an inch, I'll snap out of the moment and it'll all be a dream.

His hoarse moan echoes throughout the small space causing my nipples to harden beneath the cotton of my bra.

"Fuuuck," he hisses. Desire pools low in my belly, and for a second, I wonder if he realizes I'm still in the room.

The thought that maybe I'm watching something I shouldn't be creeps into my mind, then my name passes his lips. The sound of arousal is thick in his voice, forcing my thighs together, desperately seeking friction.

"You like watching me?"

An air of arrogance discernable in his tone forces my jaw to tighten. I grit my teeth knowing he's enjoying teasing me. Every single day he's tempting me, pushing me until I'll inevitably crack.

"You like the thought of me touching myself while I think of you?"

If he thinks I'm going to admit it to him, he can go to hell. I want to snap myself out of my stupor and demand myself to leave.

It's not worth playing whatever game he's playing. Try again.

"What if I told you I've jerked off thinking about you damn near every night since you've moved in?"

Forcing a heavy breath, my eyes flutter shut, picturing him lying in his bed, his underwear pulled down below his hips and his fist wrapped around himself. My name on his lips as his hips piston, pushing himself over the edge when he cums.

I cross my leg over the other, trying but failing to ease the desire pulsing through me. I'm seconds away from unbuttoning the front of my shorts, but I won't. It feels like I'd be surrendering to him.

I won't give in to him or the temptation.

"I can see you, ya know? You can try to play it off like you're not interested, but I see how you're fighting this as much as I am. Are you sure you don't want to take off your pants? You can slide up on the edge of the sink and spread those sexy legs for me."

His breath gets caught at the mention of me spreading my legs open for him, and his pace begins to pick up.

Something about giving in to him snaps me out of my haze. I force my eyes away from him and push the sound of his moans reverberating through the small bathroom out of my mind. Swinging the cabinet door open, I grab my curling iron off the shelf. When I reach for the door, I hear the deep growl of my name echoing around me, weakening my resolve. Forcing my feet to move proves to be more effortful than I expected.

I race back down the hall, safely shutting the bedroom door behind me. I slump against the hardwood, trying to push the images out of my mind.

I cannot believe what just happened.

Even more, I can't believe I wanted it. I've hated Brix Ward since I was twelve years old, and the thoughts I've had about him over the last week have me questioning who the hell I am and what is wrong with me.

Later that night, I'm busting my ass at Whiskey Barrel. It's a weeknight and we're still understaffed, so Jayde has Oaklyn and me handling the bar while she waitresses. It's not until after eight when business finally starts to die down and I'm grateful because I'm rockin' a terrible headache that won't seem to quit.

I slip into the back room, grabbing the small bottle of ibuprofen I keep in my purse for the nights spent studying when my head won't stop pounding. Realizing I forgot my water at the bar, I rush back to the front in search of something to help me send this thing straight back to hell.

Unscrewing the cap, I shake a couple tablets into my hand and toss them into my mouth along with some water, swallowing them down.

"You should try nuts. They help, too."

Glancing up, my eyes fall on a tall, stocky man. He looks familiar, my eyes narrow trying to figure out where we've met. He's broad, the kind you'd want playing on your football team. If you saw him coming at you, you'd want to make sure you have on some heavy padding because he'd do some serious damage.

"Excuse me?"

"Nuts," he says, motioning to the bottle still in my hand. It must be the dumbfounded look on my face that shows I'm utterly confused. He blushes, peering down at his folded hands resting on top of the bar, laughing.

"Sorry, they help with headaches."

"Seriously?"

"Seriously." He nods. "Almonds specifically. You should try it sometime."

I chuckle. "Thank you, I will. You thirsty? Can I get you anything?"

Swiping the towel from my back pocket, I go about wiping down the counter as he stares at me. His eyes flit down to the end of the bar. He seems anxious or nervous, causing the muscles in his forearms to tense.

"I'm not looking to order anything, actually. I just finished eating with some buddies not too long ago." He gestures over his shoulder. A group of guys from a table near the back are staring at the two of us. They smile while waving playfully before my eyes fall back on him. "I just wanted to talk to you."

"You did?" I giggle at how clearly staged this is, yet still taken by surprise. "We went to school together, right?"

I recognize some of the guys he's with from high school. He looks different than I remember, not sure if I can recall his name. Although I must say, we're not the same people we were back then.

"Yeah, we did. Ivy, right?"

He smiles. It's the type of warm smile that would make any girl giddy.

I nod. "Trevor," I say, his name finally hitting me.

He nods, too. "I've seen you around here a couple of times. I was wondering if you would be interested in going out sometime?"

Staring at Trevor, I take in his strawberry-blond waves, looking a little disheveled but in a boy next door sort of way. His green eyes are bright, a smile plastered on his face waiting for me to answer.

He's the exact opposite of Brix, right down to the sweet way he offered advice to fight my headache. He's everything you should want in a man.

He's also not my stepbrother.

Before I can even second-guess it, the words are out of my mouth, taking us both by surprise.

"I'd love to."

He grins, the nervousness he wore a moment ago vanishes.

He smacks his hand down on the counter with excitement, moving to stand. I realize now how much taller he is compared to me, standing over a foot taller than I do.

He pulls out his phone, and I rattle off my number. My phone vibrates in my pocket when he mentions he's going to send me a quick text so I'll have his. Before I know it, he's heading back to rejoin his friends with the promise to text me tomorrow to make plans.

It's been over a year since I've been on an actual date. His excitement and enthusiasm, once I agreed, give me reassurance we'll have a fun time.

I watch Trevor weave through the crowd of people, waving at me over his shoulder before he goes.

As he disappears from my sight, my eyes fall back to the stage toward the front of the bar, the same stage I've watched Brix and A Rebels Havoc play, and just like that, my mind is back on him.

I tell myself over and over, not to overthink it. Maybe this will be a good thing, and it'll help convince Brix to leave me alone, at least for a while.

Lies. More and more lies.

CHAPTER SEVEN

IVY

I'm regretting my decision to go on this date. It has nothing to do with Trevor. On paper, he's the definition of the perfect guy. The type you'd want to bring home to introduce to your parents, knowing they'd love him for you for all the same reasons.

The only thing missing is the connection.

I hate how it's even a comparison. It shouldn't even be a thought in my mind right now, but the attraction and pull I experience around Trevor doesn't compare to what I feel around Brix.

This is ludicrous. I'm an insane fool.

Why am I comparing him to that self-absorbed asshole?

It's the glimpses I see of Brix being a nice person that has me questioning every negative thought I've had about him since he walked back into my life. As soon as the belief enters my mind, it's quickly batted out by him being a complete jackass the next.

The doorbell rings, and I turn off my curling wand while giving myself one last look in the mirror. Grabbing my purse, I hit the light before jogging down the stairs toward the front door.

I swing the door open at the same moment Trevor reaches for the doorbell once more.

"Oh, there you are. For a second, I was wondering if I had the right house."

"Sorry, just a few last-minute touch-ups." I smile, swinging my purse over my head to sit at my hip. Tucking my hair behind my ear, I snag my keys to lock the door. Trevor stands out on the front porch stoop, waiting.

"I didn't know you lived here. Isn't this Brix Ward's house?"

"Yep," I say with a pop, "he's my stepbrother."

Even saying the words out loud sound foreign on my lips. It's the truth, he is, but it seems weird to admit.

"I had no idea." His eyes widen, surprised.

"It's okay. It's all very recent, actually. I was just as shocked as you are."

He presses his hand on my lower back, escorting me to his car, a sleek, black BMW.

Another check for him. Clearly, he has his shit together. Even standing next to him, I feel out of place.

It's obvious we live vastly different lives. I push the thought out of my mind, though, telling myself I'm going to ignore any inklings this may not be a good idea and enjoy the night. It's a date, not marriage. It's not that serious.

He's dressed in a charcoal-colored V-neck t-shirt and denim shorts, paired with gray loafers. Casual but comfortable for what our date has planned. It's been years since I've been home for the annual Sweet Summer Festival.

They have rides, games, and raffles. I heard Jayde mention last night that A Rebels Havoc is on deck to play in the beer tent. For all I know, they could be here tonight since I never bothered to pay attention to when it would be.

We walk around the festival first, hitting a few rides before checking out the games. Despite my hesitation at the beginning of the evening, now that I'm here, I'm glad I decided to go. I've been working a lot of long nights. Although a part of me wanted to hang out and veg at home, I'm happy I came.

"Want to race?" Trevor grins, pointing to the water gun game.

"Are you sure?" I ask, raising my brow at him. His eyes narrow for a moment, questioning me. "I mean, this is our first date. What if you lose? How will you recover?"

He tosses his head back, laughing. His hair bounces with each chuckle.

Crossing my arms, I hitch my hip and roll my eyes, showing how unamused I am by his reaction.

He goes stone-faced when he sees I'm serious, despite the small smirk fighting the urge to curve his mouth.

"I'm sure," he boasts, confidently, "the real question is what am I going to get when I win?"

"Typical male. Always thinking about what they get in return. As if the title of the winner isn't enough?"

"Oh, I'll gladly take the title. I have something else I want to claim as well."

"What would that be exactly?"

"I'll tell you when I beat you. How about that?"

"Well, alright. If you say so."

We both wait as the round in front of us finishes before claiming the two seats on the end. Trevor tosses two five-dollar bills on the counter, rolling his shoulders back, loosening up before it's our turn.

I don't pay him any mind at this point. I'm focused, ready to rumble. Wrapping my hands around the handles, I lean in to adjust my eye level with the pointer, waiting for the signal to start.

Right when the shot fires off announcing our start, I hear Brix's voice behind me knocking my focus off-kilter.

Shoving all thoughts of him out of my mind, I hit the trigger and aim the water at the hole, pushing my boat along. My eyes bounce from mine to Trevor's, and he's just barely behind me.

"You're going down, Trev!" I shout over the music.

"Not happening!" he yells, leaning in closer to adjust his aim as my boat crosses the finish line, sending the buzzer ringing.

Spinning around in my seat, I recline back on my elbows with a smug grin on my face. Holding a finger gun in the air, I shoot a fake shot before blowing on the end of the barrel.

"Told ya." I smirk, winking at Trevor.

I collect my prize from the row of teddy bears and useless trinkets. Tucking the small tie-dye bear under my arm, I jump down from the platform and come face-to-face with Brix and his group of friends.

His foot is propped up against the cement wall a few feet across from us. The stark contrast between him and

Trevor dawns on me. He's dressed all in black—denim jeans, a t-shirt, and Chuck Taylors. Sunglasses cover his eyes and his trademark silver chain hangs from his pocket. His slicked-back hair ties it all together, giving the impression as though he just stepped off the set of Grease.

My eyes fall on the lip ring he has clamped between his teeth. My mind immediately escapes to the thought of biting his lip and sucking it into my mouth.

As if reading my thoughts, a small smile curves on his mouth, sliding his sunglasses off his face and tucking them into the collar of his shirt. His eyes rake over my body, stopping at the black gladiator sandals wrapped around my feet. He pauses on my legs, up to my chest, until his eyes meet mine once more.

Trevor's palm presses against my lower back, pulling me out of the moment, and it's then when Brix connects the dots on who I'm here with. The features on his face completely change. What was once sexy and playful has now turned into something much darker and more sinister. If I didn't know better, I'd say he is pissed or maybe even jealous.

Why would he be?

"Out on a date so soon, sister?"

I feel Trevor's hand tense against my back.

"Shut the hell up, Brix," I warn. "Ignore him," I mutter under my breath to Trevor. "Let's go. Do you want to hit one of the rides?"

"What about how you came into the bathroom the other day when you knew I was showering?"

Heat flares up my neck. If it weren't for all the people around, I'd kill him right here. I'd go to jail for murder, and I wouldn't even feel bad about it for a second.

"That's not how it happened, and you know it."

Even though it is, and the scent of the lies hangs over my head, I feel Trevor's fingers dig into my back.

"You mean to tell me you didn't stand there and watch me while I showered?"

"Go to hell, Brix."

A salacious grin takes over his face, and I so badly want to smack it off.

"Let's go," I respond harshly. I feel my blood boiling, the anger and adrenaline rising. The crowd of people and their eyes on me leave me feeling like I'm standing butt naked in front of them.

I'm going to make Brix pay for this. I don't know how or when, but I'll make him regret this one day.

Trevor doesn't say anything when I storm off, but he eventually catches up to me. In my haste to get away, I dropped the bear on the ground.

He holds the stuffed animal out to me. Swiping it from him, I toss it into the garbage can a few feet in front of us, marching across the makeshift park toward his car.

"I'm sorry, Trevor. I think I'm ready to go home now."

"What? Ivy, no! Don't let him get to you. I didn't believe a thing he said. Brix is a jackass, okay. I've known that since I first met him. Don't let him ruin our night."

I stop, crossing my arms over my chest using one of my hands to massage my forehead as if my fingers can somehow erase the embarrassment and anger I felt a moment ago.

"I'm just in a bad mood now. Can we find something else to do?"

"Yeah, sure. Whatever you want. You won, after all. You can call the shots for the rest of the night."

After we leave, Trevor drives us down by the beach. We stop for a snow cone before going for a walk. I'm not able to pull my mind from what happened, and it causes a sinking feeling in my chest. I know Trevor sees it. He doesn't even act surprised when I tell him I'm ready to head home early. Disappointment blankets his face, but always the gentleman, he doesn't protest while he walks me to his car and drives me home.

Brix is nowhere in sight when he drops me off and walks me to the door. I'm grateful he doesn't make a move to try to kiss me. After we say our goodbyes, he promises to text me tomorrow and leaves me with a warm hug, telling me to have a good night. All my energy has been drained from me. Once inside, I head straight for my bathroom to clean up and get ready for bed. I keep the light off when I change my clothes, pulling on a t-shirt before crawling into bed.

I'm asleep before my head even hits the pillow. The sound of someone stumbling up the stairs wakes me a little while later. Pulling my phone out from where I tucked it under my pillow, the time reads after one in the morning.

I'm about to roll over and fall back asleep when the soft, giggling sounds of a woman filters through the door. The heavy weight in my chest returns, causing my heart to sink further.

Brix is home, and he's not alone.

Their muffled words mixed with his moans and her giggles has my heart aching more. When his door shuts and his stereo flips on, I'm momentarily relieved for the sound of the music distracting from the torture of listening to them, until my thoughts shift to what they're doing.

I picture him touching her in all the ways he's talked about touching me—his mouth on hers as he grips her body, his hips moving against her when he brings them both to the precipice of their release.

Except, it's not some faceless woman I see in my mind. Every thrust, every kiss, every moan is for me.

This is his way of trying to get back at me for tonight, to drive the knife even deeper, but even I know it's not her he's fucking.

It's me.

CHAPTER EIGHT

BRIX

The first thing I notice waking up the next morning is warm breath on my face mixed with the subtle sound of snoring. Immediately, I'm awake and ready for whoever is passed out in my bed to get out of here.

I don't even try to be patient or careful as I pull my arm out from under the blonde sleeping next to me. Her wild curls in disarray toss haphazardly all over my pillow. She's naked, except for the black bra still covering her chest. We hadn't got quite that far.

I'm a legs and ass man, to be honest, so it wasn't on the top of my priorities. I hadn't planned or expected this to turn into a slumber party. When we got back to my place and into my room, I had to toss back a couple shots of Jack Daniel's to push the look on Ivy's face at the fair out of my mind.

I saw the shoes she wore by the door when we came stumbling in, but her bedroom door was closed. She had to have heard us last night. In fact, that was the whole plan of this rendezvous in the first place.

Like I said, I still hadn't expected her to sleep over. Now that I'm awake, rocking a wretched hangover, I'm ready for her to get out of here so I can sleep this off alone.

"Time to wake up!" I shout over my stereo still playing. I reach for my discarded t-shirt, pulling it over my head.

She groans, rolling over and curling her arm under her head. I stare at her sleeping form, realizing this is going to be more difficult than I had initially thought.

Padding my way over to the other side of the room, I toss open the room-darkening curtains and pull up the blinds. She throws an arm over her face, groaning once more.

"C'mon. I need you to go now. I'm ordering you an Uber."

Picking up my phone, I pull up the app and tap the request for an Uber to take her back to her car at the fairgrounds. It finally takes ripping the blanket off her before she wakes up. It's cold in here. I hate sleeping when it's hot, so I know with her butt-naked ass on display, it can't be comfortable.

"You could've let me sleep. I could've seen myself out."

I chuckle. If she thinks I'd let her sleep without me here, she's fucking crazy.

"Yeah, not gonna happen. I need ya to go, now."

She slips on her pants, not bothering with underwear, and pulls her tank top over her head. I realize now, she must not have worn panties in the first place.

Opening the door to my room, I wait before I follow her down the stairs. I notice Ivy's door is open as we pass by, but she's nowhere in sight. When I checked the time a few minutes ago, it was shortly after eight, so she must be up already.

Our parents took off to stay at our beach house near Myrtle Beach for the weekend. It's a couple of hours away from Carolina Beach. They haven't really been around much since they got home from their impromptu wedding. My dad often stays at his loft in the city since it's close to work. Charlene has been staying there with him, wanting more time together now that they're married.

Shaking my head, I still can't believe all this has happened. It feels like everything over the past few weeks has been a dream. It hardly seems real that the girl I grew up hating is somehow my sister.

*Step*sister, I clarify to myself. 'Cause there is nothing pure about the thoughts I've been having about her since she walked back into my life.

Passing by the kitchen, I hear the refrigerator slam shut as my phone vibrates in my pocket. Checking the screen, there's a notification signaling the Uber is here.

Right on time.

Opening the door, I don't bother to say anything, staring directly ahead at the woman who's had me in knots since the moment she waltzed back into my life. Blondie makes a comment about enjoying herself last night, but I don't even take my eyes off Ivy.

She's holding a blender cup in her hand containing what looks like a smoothie, dressed in a pair of black workout leggings and matching sports bra.

"Are you even going to walk me out?" Blondie asks.

Looking over at her, straight-faced, I respond, "Wasn't planning on it."

"You're not even going to ask for my number?"

"Nope."

She drops her jaw, shocked I'd have the audacity to deny her request. What's the point? I have no point in using it. Why would I give her false hope?

"You're a jackass," she sneers, stepping out onto the front porch.

"I could've told ya that one," I retort, slamming the door shut behind her.

"Wow." Ivy laughs, but there's not even an ounce of surprise on her face. "You really are a prick."

"Don't tell me it took this long for you to figure it out."

"Oh, no. I've known this since we were in ninth grade and you told the new kid, Skyler, I stuffed my bra."

I laugh, but the mention of her bra has me very much aware of what she is wearing now. Gauging by how tight hers is, fitting her like a fucking glove, there's no denying what she is working with is all real.

Her stomach flexes, showing the indent of her abs. She's in killer fucking shape. I'm damn near ready to ask her to turn around so I can get a good look at her ass in those pants.

"I'm sad to see your boyfriend isn't here this morning."

"I know you were a little distracted and obviously carried away last night, but he dropped me off and went home. You know, like a gentleman would after a first date."

"Oh, a gentleman, huh?"

She holds her cup in front of her mouth ready to take a drink as if second-guessing her answer before she replies.

"Yeah, gauging by how you walked your date out this morning, that's clearly something you know nothin' about."

Eliminating the distance between us, I move in close enough to where I bump into her arm. She narrows her eyes at me, moving to slide the cup onto the counter away from us, anticipating what's about to come next.

She smells like a fresh scent mixed with the subtle smell of chocolate. I'm tempted to lean in closer but judging by the heavy rise and fall of her chest, being this close to her now is earning me the reaction I was hoping for.

She takes a step back, pressing the small of her back against the edge of the counter. Grasping the edge of the granite with both my hands on either side of her, her eyes search my face waiting for what I'm about to do.

Her chest is pressed against mine now, and I can feel my dick harden in my pants. I want to lean back and see if her nipples are beading beneath the material, want to run my fingers over the soft skin of her stomach, holding her against me.

My breath feathers across her ear, earning me a shiver, but she doesn't push me away.

"You can sit here and tell me he's the kind of guy you want. You may even have yourself convinced he's the perfect man for you. Still doesn't change the fact when you're lying in your bed, rubbing your fingers over that sweet pussy, it's me you're thinking about."

She rears her head back, fire blazing in her eyes. I'm waiting for her to fight me on it, but the argument never comes.

"Did it turn you on lying in your bed last night, listening to me make her cum?"

"Excuse me?" she asks, stumbling over her words.

"Did you picture it was you I was touching while you lay there, listening as I fucked her? Were you wet at the thought of what it would be like if I were to touch you?"

"Actually, I put in earbuds and turned on my music, so I didn't have to listen to you."

Her face flushes, forcing a thick swallow. She's lying, but I give her an A for effort.

"Try again."

"What?"

"If you think I'm actually going to believe that, you'll need to try again."

She doesn't say anything. Judging by the look of desire in her eyes, it's clear I've won this round.

"What about after the day when you watched me in the shower? Did you lie in your bed that night and rub your pussy, thinking about how I made myself cum watching you?"

"You're disgusting."

Moaning, I whisper, "Yes, I'm very dirty. Answer me."

"Leave me alone, Brix. I'm not doing this with you."

"Tell me I'm right, and I will."

"I said I'm not doing this with you. Now, GO!" Pushing me back, she shoulders past me and stomps toward the entryway, snatching her purse from where it sits on the bench seat.

"What do I owe you?"

She reaches into her wallet and yanks out a handful of cash, clenching it into a fist.

"Owe me for what?"

“Don’t play stupid with me, Brix. I’m done playing these games. What do I owe you for the car? I want to pay you back and be done.”

Clenching my jaw, I shake my head, stalking toward the fridge. Jerking the door open, I reach for a bottle of water. Unscrewing the top, I force myself to take a drink before I even try to rationalize with her.

“Brix, I’m serious.” Her tone is growing angrier.

“I’m not takin’ your fuckin’ money. You thanked me for it. Why you bringin’ this shit up again?”

“If I have to live with you for the rest of the summer, I don’t want it to be with this hanging over my head.”

“Who’s hangin’ this shit over your head, Ivy?”

“It’s just, I mean, if I’m going to live here and we have to be around each other, I want to not feel guilty about it. I’m not looking for some handout. The shit you said about my mom. I don’t know who you think we are, but I’m not looking to take either your or your dad’s money.”

Is that what she thinks? That she’s here looking for some handout? It’s never even crossed my mind.

Yeah, she came home to stay with her mom for the summer. I also happen to know she’s been busting her ass back at school. Before I knew who Ivyana, the daughter of Charlene, was, I knew all about her accomplishments. My dad hasn’t always been proud of the path I’ve chosen, but he was proud of hers. He says a musician’s life is unpredictable, and I’m throwing away my life on something that may never work out.

It’s how I know this isn’t about the money for her. She could easily take a handout from her mom, live a comfortable life while she focuses on school next year.

Except she's not. She's putting in the work, and if anything, it makes me respect her even more.

"I'm not hangin' nothin' over your head. I don't do shit I don't wanna do, Ivy. You hear me? I did it because I wanted to help you. You already said thank you. Can we move the fuck on now?"

She stares at me for a moment, evidently not expecting the anger I threw back. I can't be pissed at her for it, though. I haven't exactly been kind to her over the years, of course, she's gonna think the worst of me.

A pang of guilt hits me in the chest.

"Thank you, Brix."

My only response is a head nod. She already thanked me, but if it makes her feel better to say it again, I'm not going to harp on it.

Stalking through the kitchen, her purse swings behind her with every step she takes, swiping her drink off the counter. With her hand on the doorknob, she pauses, releasing a heavy breath before she turns her head to face me.

"I think there's a good person hidden underneath this asshole exterior you show to the world. I wish you'd show more of him because I kind of like him."

Without another word, she opens the door and walks out, leaving me alone with nothing but my thoughts and my own guilt.

CHAPTER NINE

IVY

"I'm meeting someone here under the name Kyla?"

The hostess flashes me a warm smile and nods, scanning over the list of names on the screen in front of her.

"Right this way." Motioning over her shoulder, she guides me through the restaurant. It's the middle of the day on a weekday and less crowded, with people scattered throughout. We pass through the bar area, across another doorway leading to another section of tables.

I spot Kyla right away, her purple hair standing out like a neon sign amongst the small group of people.

"The server will be right with you," the hostess says, as I slide into the seat across from Kyla.

Her fingers had been fast at work, skating across her screen. She smiles to herself, apparently at a message she had sent, before setting her phone down.

"Long time no talk, woman! I've missed you. You're always working. We need to hang out more, and soon."

"I know," I sigh, sagging back against the seat.

So much has happened since I got home that I've been meaning to catch her up on. She must sense there's a lot on my mind when she says, "Spill it, woman. Tell me what's going on."

"Well, I told you about how my car broke down and how Brix had stopped to give me a ride?"

She nods.

"I woke up the next morning to a phone call from Miller's Auto. I guess Brix, at some point, made a call to have my car towed in. I have no idea when or why. I was hardly up before they told me it was fixed, and I could come to pick it up."

"He did what?" Her eyes bug out of her head, smacking her hand on the table.

My thoughts exactly. When has Brix ever done a nice thing for anyone?

"Right? I couldn't believe it. Despite some rude shit he said to me at the bar earlier that night, which he kind of apologized for, I guess I thought we were moving past it, ya know? Until he decided to bring some girl home last night."

Kyla's eyes narrow, staring at me for a moment with confusion etching her brow. I want to tell her it's doesn't bother me like she thinks it does. By the look in her eyes, any line I try to spin to convince her won't matter.

"He kept me up all night with the sound of her yelping and his headboard banging against the wall. At least he had the courtesy of *trying* to cover it up with his music blaring."

Kyla chuckles.

"I didn't find it funny at all," I huff, rolling my eyes. "It went on for *three frickin' hours.*"

She takes a drink of her water, studying me as she sets the glass down between us.

"What is it about him bringing someone home that bothers you?"

"Well, for one, I was trying to sleep."

She nods.

"Secondly, it's disgusting. He walked her out this morning and didn't even know her name."

"This is Brix we are talking about. He's never been one for hearts and flowers. I think most of the women who hook up with him know it, too."

"It doesn't give him an excuse to treat people that way."

"Are you more upset by the fact he kept you up last night or that he slept with someone?"

To answer her truthfully, all of it. It seemed like he only brought her home to toy with me. Part of me knew he was trying to get back at me for Trevor. He was pushing my buttons, trying to get under my skin. He thought by bringing her home and fucking her against our paper-thin walls, he was going to hurt me.

I don't know why, but it was that fact that bothered me the most.

"All of it," I admit, ripping the paper off the end of my straw, shoving it into my ice water. I avoid her eye contact, leaning forward to take a drink, focusing on cars driving by on the busy street outside.

Kyla knows me well enough to know I don't want to talk about it anymore, and I think we are both thankful when our waitress approaches to take our order.

Kyla folds her menu, handing it to the server when her phone beeps from where it's sitting on the table. Glancing down, I spot a notification flash on her screen from Tysin. She quickly grabs her phone, but not before I see who it's from.

"I'll have your food right out," the waitress says.

As soon as she's out of earshot, I turn the tables on Kyla.

"Spill it," I say, mimicking her as I point to her phone.

She ignores me, looking down at the screen to check the message before setting it face down on the table.

I stare at Kyla, waiting for her response. She'll squeeze me like a pimple until I'm ready to pop when she wants to get information out of me, but when I do the same, she's stone-faced. I stare at her, taking in the black hoop in her nose to the diamond studs in her ears, while I wait.

"It's nothing really," she mutters. Her shoulders sag, looking defeated. A hint of longing coats her voice, and I know from growing up watching her every time Tysin came around, she wished it wasn't the case.

"Well, he's texting you, so that has to mean something."

"He's been coming down to Breaking Waves lately." She shrugs. "We've talked a few times, but I don't know what's going on."

Kyla's been working at the local surf shop near the boardwalk. I hadn't pegged Tysin as a surfer. None of the guys in A Rebels Havoc are, but apparently, it doesn't stop him from finding reasons to drop in and talk to her.

Whatever happens, we both know the moment her brother finds out, he'll put his foot down and demand it end.

"What are we doing, Ivy?"

Judging by the look on her face, she feels just as confused as I do.

"They're a pair of assholes, and we both know it's going to end in disaster."

She's right. Yet, even knowing it, when we both get up and walk out of here later, we'll be going right back to where we are now. As much as we know they're bad for us, we're going to have to find out for ourselves.

We spend the rest of our lunch talking about how my job is going and make plans to hit up the beach on my day off next week. Before we leave, we hug, and I promise to stay in touch more, before I head home, hoping to relax before my shift later that night.

The house is quiet when I get back. Brix and his truck are nowhere to be found. Jogging up the steps, I head for my room to get ready. I'm standing in the bathroom, putting on the finishing touches to my makeup, when I hear the front door open and close. Our parents are hardly around since returning from their recent trip, so my first guess is Brix.

The floor creaks with footsteps walking past the door, continuing down the hall before walking back toward me.

"Ivy?" Brix's knuckles rasp against the wood of the door.

"Yes?"

"Can I talk to you before you head out?"

I pause, wondering how he knows my work schedule, but let it go. It can't be hard to figure out what nights are busy at the bar or to notice my comings and goings.

"I guess."

"I don't want to fight with you."

"That isn't helping reassure me..."

"Just come downstairs when you're done."

"K," I respond, clipped.

I'm on hyperalert, listening for any sound of movement on the other side of the door. It's quiet for what feels like a minute before I hear the floor groan again as he walks down the steps.

Letting out a deep exhale, I stare at myself in the mirror, picking up the tube of mascara, I take my time doing the rest of my makeup, in hopes of delaying whatever conversation we're about to have.

When I'm certain I've wasted enough time, I pick up the rest of my stuff and put it back into the linen closet before turning off the light.

I opted to wear my hair down tonight and kept it light on the makeup, only a small amount of champagne-colored eyeshadow and mascara.

Dressed in my Whiskey Barrel tank top and denim shorts, I grab a pair of socks to wear with my sneakers and drag myself downstairs. The sliding glass door is open, leading out onto the back patio, and the scent of food cooking on the grill permeates the air.

"Hey," I say, holding my hand against the door frame. Brix's back is facing me, his shirt pulled off, hanging over his shoulder. He's barefoot, dressed in only a pair of black shorts with the chain clipped to his wallet in his back pocket.

He glances over his shoulder, his eyes falling on my chest, pausing on my legs before they finally meet mine. He pulls his lip ring into his mouth, biting down.

"Hi," he replies, turning his attention back to the food.

"What did you want to talk about?"

Stepping down onto the patio, the concrete is warm against my bare feet, as I take a seat on the lawn chair, facing him.

"You hungry?"

"What?"

"Food." He motions to the burgers cooking on the grill. "You want some?"

I'm still full from lunch with Kyla, shaking my head no. I can't help but feel like this is some sort of peace offering.

He doesn't say anything, turning back to flip the rest of the burgers before setting the spatula down on the table and ducks back into the house.

A few minutes later, he steps outside with plates in his hand and condiments in the other. His arms are full, and even though I declined his invitation, I jump to my feet to help him, but he pulls back, shaking his head.

"Just sit."

Pressing my lips together, I drop my arms to my sides and suppress the urge to speak my mind. My tongue darts out, wetting my dry lips. His eyes fall on my mouth, watching as I do. When my teeth clamp down on my lower lip, dragging it into my mouth, his eyes look back at me once again.

Shaking his head, he stalks away from me and sets everything down on the patio table next to us. His movements are shaky, something clearly bothering him. The ceramic makes a clattering sound against the glass tabletop before he resumes checking the food.

Why does he have to be so frustrating? If he's not going to say anything, what's the point of him saying he wanted to talk to me?

I have less than an hour before I leave for my shift, and I don't want to spend the rest of my time skating around whatever is on his mind. I decide then to cut to the chase.

"Do you wanna tell me what exactly you wanted to discuss?"

"You can't just chill, can you?"

"Brix," I retort, void of any emotion at all. I'm sick of the fucking games.

He must tell by the tone of my voice he's pissing me off.

"I wanted to make some fuckin' food and forget all the bullshit that's happened. Can we do that?"

"And what, forget all the shit you've said and done to me?"

"Well... yeah?"

"NO! Just no, Brix! You can't do one or two nice things and expect me to suddenly forget the many shitty things you've said and done."

"Why not?"

"Are you kidding? Because no matter what you say, your actions have always said differently. It's like you get off on fucking with me."

He tosses the spatula on the table. The sound of the metal clanging against the glass table startling me. He stalks toward me, his face red with anger and his breath heavy with every step he makes.

He bends forward, pushing himself into my space, forcing me to lean away from him.

"Why do you always have to push my fucking buttons?" His nostrils flare.

"Why do you always have to be an asshole?"

"I can't change who I am."

"Well, then I can't change the fact I hate you either."

He grimaces, swallowing hard, and I immediately want to take back those words. Even when they come out of my mouth, I know I don't mean them.

He takes a step away from me, crossing his arms in front of his chest. Somewhere along the way, he dropped his shirt on the floor. His muscles clench, his jaw set.

"Brix, I didn't..."

"Just don't. Forget it."

"Oh, so now you don't want to talk?"

He doesn't respond.

"We're going to have to deal with one another for the rest of the summer. Alright? It's not like we're going to be able to avoid each other. We have to figure out a way to put this aside," I say, holding my arms out.

"Fine! We'll avoid each other. You go your way, I'll go mine. We'll go back to living like the other doesn't exist."

Why does it feel like he reached into my chest and ripped my heart out? It shouldn't bother me, but it does. If he's trying to change my mind about him, he's giving in a lot easier than I thought he would've.

I'm not about to let him start getting to me now.

Pushing all hurt aside, I give him the only response I can at the moment, and that's not a single word. Turning on my heel, I walk back into the house, effectively ending the conversation and any possibility of the two of us getting along.

CHAPTER TEN

BRIX

The days after we agree to stay out of each other's way are void of Ivy's presence. I can only assume she's taken off and decided to stay with Kyla or another friend. The house is empty with our parents jet-setting off to Aruba, deciding now is the perfect time to take their honeymoon, leaving me with mixed feelings of the quietness surrounding me.

You'd think with them married and now taking off to celebrate, the reality of the situation would set in, and I'd find a way to get over the thoughts of Ivy that've plagued me. What started off as fucking with her has quickly turned into something else.

The tension between us has grown. That, combined with the way I can't seem to think straight when she's near, the way my dick grows hard being around her, and the dreams of ravaging her keeping me up at night. I need to find a way to accept this simply cannot happen with us.

No matter how I feel about her, she's my stepsister. Giving in to the desires, whether it's to fuck with her or not, would be too messy. Being close to Ivy is like dodging a landmine. If I get too close to her, we're going down together.

I meet up with Tysin and Madden early that afternoon for band practice. It's rough; Tysin's constantly checking his phone. Whatever he's texting someone about can't possibly be good, and the fact we're both distracted puts Madden in a bad mood. We each have a lot on our minds, so we decide to call it an early night.

It's Wednesday, which happens to be the night I know Ivy doesn't usually work. Something about knowing she'll be off tonight has me hoping she'll finally stop the cat and mouse games and come home.

Home. Why the fuck am I thinking about it like we live here, together? Like this is more than what it is?

After band practice, we head over to the Shake Shop. Most of our friends hang out down by the beach during the summer. With the Shake Shop sitting off the pier, it makes it a hoppin' place even on a weeknight.

The sun has started to set when we pull up. Tysin's in the front seat across from me, Madden sitting in the truck bed of my '69 Chevy.

As soon as I put it in park, Tysin's door is open, and Madden makes the jump over the side of the truck.

"You fuckers can't even wait until I have the thing turned off, can you?"

Madden doesn't even acknowledge me, and Tysin holds his middle finger over his head.

I'm not in the mood to eat. With my leg perched beneath me, I lean against the wall with my arms crossed in front of my chest. Sunglasses shield my eyes, watching the beach-goers pass by us along the boardwalk.

"Will you put on some clothes?" Madden barks.

Glancing over, I spot his sister approach with her friends following along behind her. She's dressed in a yellow bikini top, and crop shorts rolled at her hips, showing off her sun-kissed skin. With her bright hair and swimsuit, there's no missing her, and now I understand Madden's comment.

Even if she's Madden's sister, she looks damn good, and I'd be a fucking liar if I said I didn't look twice.

It doesn't take long though before my eyes are trailing away from her to the brunette standing behind her. Ivy's deep brown hair is down, pulled over her shoulder. The bright red swimsuit top with matching wrap sitting low on her hips.

When I say low, I mean fucking *low*, showing off her hip bone. Immediately, my mind trails to what she is covering beneath those small bikini bottoms and see-through sarong.

Once again, thoughts of Ivy seep into my mind like a fucking poison out to kill me slowly. I imagine what she'd look like spread out before me on my bed. Her wild hair fanning around her as I slip off her sexy-as-sin swimsuit and taste her.

The thought of how sweet she would be makes my mouth water. Dragging myself from the visions flashing through my mind to find the spotlight of my dreams standing in front of me.

I don't take my eyes off her, even when she shoots daggers at me, remembering how she spoke to me the last time we saw each other.

At least until I notice Frankenstein standing behind her. I don't know what it is she sees in this guy. Dude looks so tense walking next to her; you'd think he had a stick shoved far up his ass.

"Well, if it isn't the three stooges," Kyla jokes, rolling her eyes at her brother before peering back over at Tysin, holding his stare. I'm waiting for Madden to knock his head off with the way he's gazing at his sister, biting his lip as he does.

"Did you see who's with Kyla?" Tysin asks, elbowing me in the side, pointing at Ivy. As if she doesn't see him.

"I'm not fucking blind."

"Whatever happened to you having her eat out of the palm of your hand? Have you fucked your sister yet?" Tysin laughs.

For a second, I wonder if Ivy heard him, her eyes darting over to me.

"If you don't shut the fuck up, you'll be eating sand in two seconds. You fucking hear me?"

Holding his palms up, he takes a step back. Tysin swipes his shake cup off the counter, backing away from me, lifting the straw up to his mouth with a smirk on his face. When Ivy turns to talk to Frankenstein next to her, Tysin has the nerve to waggle his brows and nod his head toward them.

Steam is practically blowing out of my ears, and I'm ready to head out of here. My eyes find Ivy once again, trying to force myself to calm down, only now it looks like she's cozied up next to him. Every so often, Ivy's eyes flit back over to mine. A few times, I don't even try to cover up the fact I'm staring back at her, too, but her eyes quickly dart away.

The moment I catch his arm draped around her waist, rubbing his thumb along the soft skin of her hip, it's time for me to jet.

"I'm about to dip out of here. You guys want a ride?" I ask, looking between Tysin and Madden, motioning to the truck.

Madden is too busy chatting it up with some girl who walked by to even pay attention. With Madden's mind in other places, Tysin's sliding in trying to talk to Kyla. He clearly doesn't want to leave now. Ivy peers over at me, surprised by my tone and abrupt decision to leave.

"Alright, I'm gonna head out," I say, looking over at Ivy. Before turning to leave, I pause and say, "I'll see you at home."

I don't wait for her to respond because truthfully, it wasn't even a question. I'm sick of her hiding and avoiding me. I'm pissed at having to watch her with this tool.

I wish we could go back to the way things were between us the night her car broke down. While it was brief, I miss the ease between the two of us.

I stop to pick up a pizza and a six-pack of beer before heading home to settle in with a movie. With all the shows we've had lately, it's been crazy, but in a good way. Sometimes I miss having laid-back, relaxing nights in or with my friends like we used to.

It's after eight, and I'm about four beers in when I stick the leftover pizza in the fridge, hearing the lock click on the front door before slowly creaking open.

I know right away it's Ivy. I intentionally locked it so I would hear when she got home.

Taking a swig of my beer, I lean against the edge of the counter and watch as she tiptoes in, kicking off her shoes in the entryway, adjusting her purse on her shoulder.

"I'm glad you finally decided to come back."

Her body tenses before she turns to face me. The apples of her cheeks are rosy, accentuating the small freckles dotting her face.

"Yeah, I bet you are."

She doesn't believe me, the smirk on her face and the hitch in her hip shows she's ready for an argument. She's waiting, armed with her sass to fire back at whatever I may throw her way.

Except she's wrong. I'm not looking for a fight with her. Not tonight.

"You care to explain Tysin's comment to me?"

I figured she heard him. The fucker knew what he was doing when he said it, too. I'm mentally making a list of all the ways I'd like to make him suffer the next time I see him.

"What comment?" I ask, playing coy.

Her eyes narrow into slits, her fist tightening around the strap of her bag, not appreciating how I'm evading the question.

I decide to ignore the daggers she's shooting at me while my eyes wander over her tanned skin, letting my eyes eat up every inch of her body still dressed in her bikini. However, she's since ditched the wrap on her waist and slipped on a pair of denim shorts with high-heel sandals that scream, "fuck me on the counter."

Now it's all I can think about.

"What was it he said again?" She pauses, before looking me in the eyes. "Have you fucked your sister yet?"

As if reading my thoughts exactly, I choke on nothing but air. My eyes water, holding my fist in front of my mouth while I struggle to breathe. A smug look passes over Ivy's face, as I take a drink to clear my throat.

Setting the empty bottle on the counter away from me, I take the two steps separating us to approach her. The move takes her off guard, and she forces a heavy breath through her nose.

I wasn't prepared for it either, as her fresh scent mixed with the smell of coconut wraps around me. My dick hardens in my shorts, straining against the zipper, fighting to break free.

"Is that what you want, Ivy?" I ask, staring down at her. "Is that why you were bothered the other night when I was with blondie? Were you jealous because I was fucking her, and you wanted it to be you?"

Her jaw is set, nostrils flaring. As anger simmers in her eyes at the mental images I'm throwing at her.

"Tell me, Ivy. Is that why you're pissed at me and have been avoiding coming back home?"

"I'm not doing this with you, Brix."

"Would it help if I told you I was picturing it was you the entire time?"

Her mouth opens slightly, taken back by my admission, but she doesn't say anything. She doesn't try to argue with me or tell me to shut up.

Just like the day in the bathroom. She stares back at me, wanting more but not admitting to herself or me it's what she wants, too.

"Does it make you feel better knowing the only way I could cum was thinking about your legs wrapped around my hips, your hands digging into my back with every thrust? It's okay if it's what you want, Ivy. I want it, too."

"I don't know what kind of game you're playing, Brix, but this isn't funny."

I can't blame her for not believing me. This is what I've done to her. I'm guilty of wanting this in the beginning for all the wrong reasons. She has every right to doubt me.

"This isn't a game, Ivyana," I say sternly. Her eyes lower at the use of her full name or maybe it's my tone.

Her stance relaxes as I step in closer, circling around her like an animal does their prey. I know I have her precisely where I want her, and the thought of taking her, consuming her, has a spike of adrenaline coursing through me.

Standing behind her, I pull her hair away from her neck, leaning in close. My dick is pressed against the curve of her ass, and I have to bite my lip to fight off the urge to moan as I subtly rock against her. With my hand against her stomach, holding her to me, she leans back into my touch.

"You feel the way my body reacts to being close to you, Ivy?" I ask, rocking against her once more. She doesn't respond, only slightly nods her head.

"Tell me you were lying in bed thinking about it, too."

Her hand covers mine at her waist, and I'm waiting for the moment she pushes me away. For a second, I think she's going to give in to me and let go of this wall she has up between us when she shoves away from me and races across the dining room and up the stairs to her room.

CHAPTER ELEVEN

IVY

Slamming the bathroom door, I sag against it until I slide down to the floor. I let the coldness of the wood cool off my heated skin as I run my hands over my face and into my hair.

Why did I let him touch me?

Why the hell am I even thinking about what he's offering?

I'm waiting for the second when I find out this is all a joke, that he's fucking with me. I don't trust Brix farther than I could throw him. If that's true, though, why is he right? Why was I lying in bed that night thinking about it being me he was with?

Standing, I open the linen closet and grab an unused washcloth. Turning the tap on the faucet, I let the cold water soak the fabric and gently press the cool cloth against my face. Turning the water off, I sit on the closed toilet seat, continuing to hold the material against my skin, helping ease the tension I'm feeling.

I can't keep running away and avoiding him. Even when he said he'd see me tonight, I knew it wasn't his way of asking if I was coming home. He was telling me either I come back tonight or he'd come find me. He was putting a stop to me ignoring him.

Now I need to figure out how I'm going to put a stop to the mess we've found ourselves in.

I sit on the toilet for longer than necessary. I listen for any sounds outside the door, any inkling he's still here or could be waiting for me.

Resigning myself to the fact I'm being a coward and need to face this head-on, I set the wet washcloth on the edge of the bathtub for when I shower in the morning and decide I'll deal with my problems tomorrow.

I'm not going to solve them all tonight and hiding in the bathroom sure as hell isn't going to fix it either.

Hitting the lock, I slowly peel open the door and step out into the hallway. As soon as I turn the corner toward my room, I see him standing at the end of the hall outside his bedroom door.

My fingers hit the light switch, and just like that, we're swallowed in darkness. The lamp from his bedroom is on, casting a faint glow from behind him. He's dressed in only shorts. His shirt is gone, and for a moment, I wish I could turn the light back on to get a better look at the tattoos covering his body.

Reminding myself of what I told myself a moment ago, I decide to not cower away anymore. Every step of the way down the hall toward my room feels like an eternity. I feel my skin burning up from the heat of his stare.

Just as I'm about to open my door, his words stop me.

"So, are you dating Frankenstein now?"

My brows furrow in confusion. "What? Who?"

"The guy at the festival? The one you were with earlier who looks like he has a stick up his ass. Are you guys together now?"

I hate to admit it, but I want to laugh at his assessment.

"No. We've been hanging out, but it's nothing serious. Nothing I see lasting beyond the summer anyway."

Peering up at him from where my hair falls in front of my face, my eyes trace his muscles from the way his arms are crossed, leaning against the doorway.

"Coulda fooled me."

"What's that supposed to mean?"

"I saw how he touched you..." He trails off. "He didn't touch you like it was the first time he had put his hands on you."

He almost sounds jealous. His reaction to me around Trevor had come off this way, but now, the words only confirm it.

"I don't think it's any of your business, Brix. I think it's best..." I let out a heavy sigh. "It's just best if we stay away from each other for the rest of the summer. Remember, you go your way, I'll go mine."

His mouth curves up, smirking. Pushing off the wall, he stalks toward me, stopping only when he gets a hair's breadth away.

"I think you're wrong. It's very much my business. I've spent every night for the past five days thinking about you while you've been avoiding me. I want you to look me in the eye and tell me you don't feel this between us."

"Brix," I whisper. "Please."

"Say it."

He grabs my hand, pulling me closer to him, and I go without argument. I don't have any strength left in me to fight this, not that I even want to anymore.

"Say what?"

His lip curves up, pushing my back against the wall. His arms wrap around my waist, his fingers dig into my skin, holding me to him.

"Do you feel this?" he asks, leaning forward until his lips are close to my neck.

Tilting my head to the side, I give him better access, waiting for the moment he puts us both out of our misery.

His hands drag up the sides of my body as he pulls back an inch, dragging his finger beneath the curve of my breast. My nipples bead at the thought of his hands touching me.

My chest starts to heave with each struggled breath; my skin heats with desire.

"Does that feel good?"

I nod, as he drags his finger up the center of my chest to the edge of my swimsuit top. The only thing covering me is two barely-there triangles held together by a couple strings.

Leaning back, I watch Brix slide his thumb in his mouth, wetting it before brushing it over the tip of my nipple.

He moans, biting down on his lip ring.

Watching his reaction to touching me has me incredibly turned on. My fingers rake over his pecs, down over his clenched stomach to the edge of his shorts. Slipping my fingers under the elastic, I wrap my fist around the waistband and pull him closer to me.

"Fuck, baby," he groans, thrusting against my stomach. His aching cock is straining through the thin material.

He doesn't hold back any longer. His fingers pull the fabric covering my chest over and it falls away without protest as his hand covers my breast.

Leaning forward, his mouth covers my nipple sending shock waves through my body at the unbelievable sensation. Gripping my fingers in his hair, I hold Brix to me, not wanting him to pull away or stop.

"Oh my God," I moan, running my palm over the front of his pants, earning me a bite on my sensitive skin.

"More. Please."

He releases my breast, immediately moving to the button on the front of my shorts. He falls to his knees before me, savagely pulling the denim to the floor, leaving me standing with only my bikini bottoms on.

"My fucking God," he mutters to himself, leaning forward to press kisses from my hip bone down over the front of the material. I thrust my hips toward him, seeking his mouth as he tilts his head back, smiling devilishly at me.

"Look at you, baby. Serving me this fucking pussy, knowing it's exactly what I want."

His vulgar words only turn me on more.

"Brix," I whisper.

"Mm, I know."

Tugging at the strings tied at my waist, my bottoms fall to the floor along with my shorts leaving me naked and exposed for him.

"Holy fuck." He presses a kiss against my upper thigh, trailing his lips over my hip bone again until he reaches my pussy. My fingers tangle in his hair, pulling him where I need him most.

Lifting my leg over his shoulder, giving him better access, he slides his tongue through my slit. His fingers digging into the curve of my ass help to stabilize me, which I'm grateful for. With nothing but my hand in his hair and my other pressed against the wall, I hold on for the glorious ride as his tongue swipes over my clit.

Rotating my hips, I ride his face like it's the one and only place I want to be. When he gently slides a finger in, my movements turn urgent while I grind against him.

"Fuck, Brix. Oh, God," I murmur, my body shaking when he adds a second finger. Once his mouth closes over my clit, sucking, the vibration from his moans sends me soaring over the edge.

Sagging against the wall, Brix grabs me by the waist. This time, he doesn't hold back, doesn't ask for permission as his mouth crashes against mine. Wrapping my hand around his neck, I hold him against me, our tongues tangling together.

Lifting me, my legs circle his waist as he carries me down the hall. My assault on his mouth doesn't slow. I'm so turned on, and all I can think about is tasting him, feeling him.

I want more of him.

He carries me into his room, dropping me on the edge of the bed. He pauses, stepping back to unbutton his shorts. Now, with the soft light filling the room, the outline of his hard dick pressing against the front of his black boxer briefs is unmistakable.

"Keep on licking your lips like that, baby, I'm going to make you take me in your mouth."

I moan at the mental image, the thought of tasting his velvety skin against my tongue, tasting his arousal.

"Fuck, is that what you want?"

He pulls down his briefs, wrapping his hand around his cock, pumping it once, twice. I'm wholly captivated watching him touch himself.

That is until I see the glistening on the tip of his dick, and it's not from pre-cum.

By the look on his face, he's enjoying me watching him while his other hand reaches down wrapping around his balls as he jerks harder, faster.

Stepping between my legs, he holds his dick out for me, and I come face-to-face with the piercing through the head of his cock. I want to ask questions, like did it hurt along with thoughts of it getting stuck in my throat, before pushing them out of my mind.

Taking him in my hand, I mimic his motions after watching what he likes. He uses his other hand to brush the hair away from my face as I lean forward and swipe my tongue beneath the head.

He responds with a string of curse words flying out of his mouth, ending with how good it feels. When he slides in my mouth, his head tilts back, and I watch in rapture the way his body winds up tight.

He thrusts his hips toward me, slowly at first, testing how far he can go. Tipping my head back, I open my mouth, giving him a subtle nod of permission to go further.

"Jesus, fuck!" he moans. I wrap my hand around the base of his cock, thrusting my hand up with him before he quickly pulls out.

With his hand clenching my hair and his head tossed back, he fucks my mouth. His moans grow louder each time he hits the back of my throat, feeling me gag around him, but I don't stop.

I never fucking stop.

"You're going to make me cum, Ivyana, and I want to feel you around me when I do."

Grabbing my hand, he pulls me so I'm standing in front of him. He pulls on the string untying the top of my bikini. Standing naked in front of him, it crosses my mind for a moment how this doesn't feel weird or uncomfortable. In fact, nothing has ever felt more right.

I don't allow myself to overthink or overanalyze all the ways this could end up a mess.

Brix takes my seat on the edge of the bed, pulling me on top of him before leaning back on his elbows. Positioning him beneath me, I rub the head of his cock over my clit.

The feel of the tip, along with the metal piercing, on my most sensitive skin, feels phenomenal.

"If you keep that shit up, I'm not going to make it much longer."

Positioning him at my core, I slowly lean back, taking in every inch. The sounds of our moans mix in the silence around us. Brix falls back on the bed, sliding his hands into mine.

We continue to rock back and forth, our heavy breaths and whispered words carrying us through each thrust. Our eyes never leave each other's, not until we both fall over the edge, crashing together until I collapse on his chest.

We lie like this for a while after we're done, me on top of him, chest to chest.

"Sleep with me?"

Reality begins to sink in. I want to pull back and question everything until I convince myself this is wrong and run away. But I don't.

Instead, we crawl under the blankets and with my head on his shoulder and his arm wrapped around me, we fall into a peaceful sleep.

CHAPTER TWELVE

IVY

Adjusting my books in my arm, I knock my shoulder against my locker, shutting it behind me, heading to History. It's my least favorite class of all, so I'm not in any hurry to get there.

My breath gets caught in my throat, startling me when I come face-to-face with Evan leaning against the burgundy lockers.

He flashes me a shy smile as I push the metal frames of my glasses up on my face.

"Sorry, didn't mean to scare you."

"It's okay," I reply nervously, "I didn't see you coming is all."

"You have Mr. Ferguson this hour, right?"

I'm surprised he even knows. I nod. "How'd you know?"

"I've been paying attention." His smile widens.

I grin, heat flushing my face. I recover quickly, trying to hide my excitement. Evan has been talking to me more often lately. At first, I wasn't sure what to think, but over the past few weeks, I've been developing feelings for him that are completely new to me. Butterflies in my stomach, shaky voice when I try to speak.

It's like all thought is out the window when he's around. I want to keep my wits about me because this boy sends me out of my mind with nerves.

"I'll walk you." He holds his hand out to lead the way.

Ducking my head down, I bite my lip to hide my grin once more. Every step we take, I'm hyperaware of each time his arm brushes mine.

"So, I've been meaning to talk to you about Homecoming next week. I was thinking." He pauses. For a second, I notice the shell in his confident exterior break, realizing whatever he's about to say is making him nervous, too. "If you don't have anyone to go with, ya know, to the dance. I'd really like to take you."

My eyes search the floor, shocked, before I glance up at Evan over the rim of my glasses. His dark hair and dark eyes looking so handsome. He stares back at me, eyes bouncing between mine down to my mouth, waiting for my response.

"Yes..." I breathe heavily. "Yes, I'd love to go to the dance with you."

We approach Ferguson's room just then and he stops, holding the door open to let me through. I cannot believe he asked me to the dance. I know we had been talking more lately, but I had no idea he had been interested in me. At least not in the same ways I was him.

"Great! I'll catch up with you, and we'll talk about all the details. See ya later, Ivy."

I nod, watching when he turns to saunter away.

Turning to head into the classroom, I'm caught off guard when I see Brix Ward leaning against the wall outside the doorway.

He chuckles, looking at me and over to Evan, whose back is facing us, each step carrying him further and further down the hall.

"What?"

"Nothing." He snickers again.

Rolling my eyes, I ignore him and focus on getting to my seat before class starts.

The days after, leading up to the dance, go by at an agonizingly slow pace. I was disappointed when Evan told me he'd meet me at the school before the dance starts, hoping he'd pick me up, like a real date. I pushed the disappointment aside and decided to focus on having a fun time.

This was my first date to a dance, well, my first date in general. Knowing it was going to be with Evan made me even happier. He had become a friend to me, and I knew it had set a foundation for what I hoped would be something great between us.

My mom took me to three different department stores the weekend before, and we shopped for hours looking for the perfect dress. As soon as I spotted the beautiful emerald-green dress on the rack, I knew it was the one for me. Green is my favorite color and one I knew not many girls would choose to wear.

Kyla and her date, Max, stand outside the building with us. The fall temperatures leaving it a little cooler, but the nerves and excitement rushing through me help add warmth to my body.

"What time did he say he'd be here?" Kyla asks, Max standing behind her with his arm around her waist. She is dressed in a stunning blue dress. The color complementing her eyes perfectly.

"Any minute now," I reply, clicking the button on the side of my phone to see the time showing ten minutes after seven o'clock.

He is late. With every minute that passes, the knot of worry sitting low in the pit of my stomach tightens.

I didn't want to think about the likelihood tonight wouldn't go as I hoped and planned.

Opening the message thread with him, I type out a response. There has to be a perfectly logical explanation for why he is late. Maybe he had car troubles, or maybe he left his corsage at home, thinking back to the beautiful rose Max had given Kyla, sitting on her wrist.

Just as I am typing out a response, a black Escalade pulls up in front of us with a line of people jumping out. My eyes fall on Brix, helping some blonde beauty out of the vehicle. Her hair and makeup flawless, her bright pink dress fitting her like a glove, making her look like a barbie doll.

I thought back to the hair my mom helped me curl. I wasn't one to normally style my hair. I usually wore my black-framed glasses to school, contacts often made my eyes itch, but for one night, I decided to get through it. Kyla helped me with my makeup. We decided to keep it minimal. I didn't want to look like I had it caked on.

Following behind Barbie, I spotted Evan sliding out of the back seat. My brows furrowed in confusion, surprised to see him hanging out with Brix and his posse of losers.

It was no secret Brix and I didn't get along. In fact, for most of my freshman year, he had made it his life's mission to make mine a living hell. Thinking back to when it all started, I can't even be sure I can pinpoint what happened or why he picked me as his proverbial punching bag.

But somewhere along the way, Brix decided he hated me and picked on me whenever he had the chance.

"Evan, hey." I smiled, waving at him to get his attention.

His eyes fell on mine, and I could see the regret on his face as he glanced down at my dress to my shoes and back up to meet my eyes.

What I expected to happen next, I have no idea, but I certainly hadn't anticipated for him to say nothing at all, which is exactly what he did. He turned, held his hand out to Barbie #2, helping her out of the Escalade. As soon as she stepped out, she adjusted her dress then wrapped her arm around Evan's.

I wish I could say I stuck it to him. That I called him out on being the biggest piece of crap at Hawk High. Anything.

I didn't, though. I ducked my head and stepped back, tears filling my eyes and threatening to fall. I managed to keep it together, as each person, one by one, climbed out of the vehicle.

"What the fuck!" Kyla shouted next to me. I should've known she would come to my rescue.

Madden, her brother, standing amongst the group, turned to look at her.

"Kyla, why don't you go find something to do besides follow me and my friends around?"

"Shut the fuck up, puke brains. You and your friends are a bunch of douchebags, you know that?"

Madden doesn't reply. He simply goes back to ignoring us, like he usually does.

When they walked past us, heading toward the front door of the school, Brix turned his head to me. The side of his lip curling up in a salacious smile, muttering, "Fucking loser."

His eyes glanced down at my dress, and immediately, I wanted to wrap my arms around me to cover myself up. His eyes traveled down the length of my body before finally falling on mine again. With nothing more than a head shake, he turned his attention back to his date.

"I'm sorry, Ivy," Kyla said, wrapping her arms around me. Once we're alone, just the three of us, I tuck my head into her neck and let the tears flow.

With the ache in my chest and the embarrassment flushing my skin, all I wanted to do was leave. I wanted to go home, take off this stupid fucking dress and drown my sorrows in a pint of Ben & Jerry's ice cream.

I wanted to forget Evan. I wanted to forget this dance.

Most of all, I wanted to forget how much I hated Brix Ward.

Something feels off before I ever open my eyes. Maybe "off" isn't the right word. Different. The heavy weight of Brix's arm wrapped around me, and the warmth of his body pressed against my back. My next thought is how heavenly this bed feels. It's what dreams are made of.

It is then that the gravity of the situation hits me.

I am naked, in bed, wrapped up in Brix Ward.

If someone would've told me at the beginning of the summer, I'd be waking up next to him after just a few weeks, I would've never believed them. Hell, I still can't believe I gave in to the temptation and desires I had felt since I moved into this house.

Peering over at the alarm clock on the nightstand, the time flashes four twenty-eight in the morning. My eyes focus on the light as my mind runs through the night before. The way he looked at me, how my body reacted to his touch, the feel of his hands and mouth on me. I don't know how anything could ever compare to being with Brix, and the realization scares me.

Despite knowing all of this, I know this won't end well, and it's the unsettling feeling that urges me to slip out of Brix's bed before the sun even starts to rise.

I need distance. I need to sort through my thoughts and feelings that are starting to consume me.

CHAPTER THIRTEEN

BRIX

I wish I could say I was surprised when I woke up the next morning to find Ivy gone. At some point in the middle of the night, she must've slipped out of bed.

Truthfully, I expected it to happen. Everything about the two of us together scared us both, beyond just the obvious reason.

She's my stepsister for fuck's sake. Doesn't change the fact my body craves hers in ways that would be viewed as unhealthy.

I wanted to ravage her, own her, make her mine.

The last part is what had me accepting she had left because if she felt even a fraction of what I did when we were together last night, it's understandable she'd need time to think.

While I knew this could end up in a disaster, it didn't stop me from hoping it'd happen again, either.

Swinging my legs over the side of the bed, I reach for my phone sitting on my bedside table as the vibration starts. I peer out one eye, I see my Uncle Travis's name flash on the screen.

What the hell could he be calling me for at seven in the morning?

"Hello?"

"Brix!" he sighs. By the tone in his voice, I know whatever he's about to say next can't possibly be good.

"Yeah?"

"I need you to get your ass over here. It's your mom," he murmurs. "She overdid it again, and, yeah. Can you get here quick?"

I'm up out of bed, pulling my shorts back on from yesterday, not bothering to sort through something to wear.

"I'll be right there."

Disconnecting the call, I snatch my black baseball cap and a Metallica t-shirt from my closet, tucking my wallet in my back pocket and head toward the door.

The last time this happened, she had to be admitted for detox for three days. Not that it really helped, but at least she was under supervision.

She assured us this wouldn't happen again. She promised she'd get help. Guilt consumes me, knowing since Ivy has started to come around, I'd been too distracted to be what she needs.

I haven't been going by her house as often, checking in on her. I failed my own mom. She needs me now, and I am going to do the best I can to be there for her. Whatever that means.

As I pass by Ivy's room, the door is shut, but something in me decides to check to see if she is here. To make sure she is okay.

Wrapping my hand around the handle, I slowly turn the knob and ease the door open. She is dressed in my black t-shirt I had left laying on my floor, the one I noticed was missing a few minutes ago, curled into a ball in the center of her bed. A small green blanket covers her legs, her bright red toes sticking out from the bottom.

She looks like an angel, sleeping peacefully. I debate taking a picture of her, wanting to remember her dressed in my shirt, but decide against it.

With my luck that would be the moment she'd wake up and catch me standing over her.

Ducking my head, I step out of her room, pulling the door shut behind me.

I have places to go and someone important to me who needs me right now. I don't have time to get caught up in the thoughts and feelings swirling around in my head. The drive over to my mom's leaves me with plenty of time to stew over them, though.

Parking in front of the small blue house, I spot my mom's broken-down Saturn. It reminds me of the old rust bucket Ivy drives. I have tried hundreds of times to get her to invest in something more reliable, but she fights me on it at every turn.

Travis steps out onto the front porch stoop, pulling a pack of cigarettes from the pocket on his button-up Miller's Auto shirt.

"She alright?"

"She's gonna be, but she needs to get help. I'm talkin' serious help, B."

"Fuck, bro. I don't know what to do."

"I'll look into it for you, but I'm talking an inpatient facility. She's gonna have to go away for a while. This can't be on you or me to help her fix it. She has to want it, and she's gonna have to do the work."

I nod. He's right. We've been trying to help her on our own for far too long. I'm beyond exhausted, and I don't know where to turn anymore.

I can't keep being the parent she should've been to me growing up. As much as I love her, I miss the mom she was to me before the divorce.

Shouldering past him, I open the screen door and step inside the house. Beer cans litter the coffee table and floor throughout the living room. Empty vodka bottles are lined up in a row on the TV stand as if being displayed like some sort of trophy.

"Brix," she slurs, holding her hand up to wave at me. "My sweet, handsome son." Her words come out like they are tied to each other. "I missed you, honey. C'mere."

She moves to sit up, holding her arms out toward me to give me a hug. Not able to say no to her, I wrap my arms around her. The strong smell of alcohol on her breath is enough to leave me drunk. I squeeze my eyes shut at the sadness that creeps over me witnessing her like this.

When is enough going to be enough?

Pulling back, she gives me a sad smile before she slumps against the couch. Her shirt is pulled up awkwardly, but she's still so drunk she doesn't even notice or maybe she doesn't care.

I grab an empty garbage bag from the kitchen, tossing empty fast food wrappers in the bag as I make my way back into the living room to pick up the stray cans on the floor and table.

"Oh, honey, you don't have to do that." She waves her hand at the mess before patting the seat next to her. "Just come sit with me, will ya?"

"Mom, you can't keep living like this."

Shoving cans into the bag, I grab the other bag I shoved into my back pocket and start filling it with the empty glass bottles, careful not to let them break as I do.

"Like what?" she asks defensively, her tone growing louder.

"You know what I'm talking about, Mom. Don't act like you don't."

"Why don't you tell me, Brix? What is the problem?"

"Look at this place!" I yell back, dropping the bag on the floor next to my feet. I hold up my arms in frustration, motioning to the mess scattered around her. "Look at the cans, bottles, fucking cigarette butts. Who the hell wants to live like this? You're drunk, and it's not even eight o'clock in the morning. Don't you see how this could be a problem?"

Rolling her eyes, she shakes her head, like she can't begin to understand how I could be upset right now.

"I'm sick of worrying whether this is going to be the time where you've gone too far. Do you want me to have to come over here and find you dead on that stupid fucking couch? Is that what you want me to have to deal with?"

Tears fill her eyes, and for a second, I wonder if maybe I've finally broken through to her.

"Of course, I don't, Brix. How could you even say that to me?"

"How could I say that? Mom, how could you do this to yourself? How could you choose this life? I've been trying to get you help for years. YEARS! What's it going to take before you finally fucking listen and accept the help?"

"Well, I'm sorry I'm such a burden to you. Okay? I'm sorry you have to deal with me and all my fucking problems. Not all of us can be as happy and perfect as your dear fucking dad."

"Don't give me that shit, Mom. C'mon." Shaking my head, I begin shoving more bottles into the bag.

"I'm going through all your shit and getting this place cleaned up. If there's an ounce of alcohol in this house, it's gone. I'm staying here with you until you sober up, and then we're checking you in somewhere. I'm not talking about some couple day detox either. I'm talkin' an actual program in an actual treatment center. It's time we get you the help you needed a long fucking time ago."

She doesn't fight me on it anymore. She stretches out on the couch, eyes closed, and her arms crossed in front of her.

It kills me to see this is what her life has come to, but I'll be damned if we will continue down this road and look back wishing I would've done more.

After everything is cleaned up, she's passed out on the couch, curled up in the fetal position. I take advantage of the chance to go through all her cabinets, all her favorite hiding places I used to discover growing up, pouring out bottles of vodka.

"It's fucked up you even know where she hides them," Travis sighs, shaking his head. He leans his hip against the counter, watching me while I pour out the final bottle.

We found some stored under the bathroom sink, behind the towels in the linen closet, even a few underneath the bottom drawer of her dresser.

That was one place I never had thought to consider until one day I found her stuffing things under there when she didn't think I was looking.

"Yeah, well, growing up with an alcoholic mom, you see things you never thought you'd see."

He nods his head, agreeing.

"A friend of mine went to this rehab center, Newhaven. Apparently, it's good. I'm waiting for the director to call me back, but it sounds like they'll be able to get her in right away. She can stay there for eight weeks; get the help she needs."

"That long?" His eyebrows shoot up, gritting his teeth.

"Yeah, man. She's not going to like it, but she needs it. After she's done, they have sober living centers and different programs available to help her with the transition back to her new day-to-day life."

Rubbing my fingers over my forehead, I massage the skin.

"Yeah, you're right. I hope she'll agree to go. She has to want this or it's pointless, just like every other time."

We stand here talking for a while before Travis takes off to pick up his daughter from her mom. They separated a few months ago and he has her every other weekend. He would never want to miss his time with her. I assure him I have it covered.

After I'm confident everything in the house is gone, I sit back on the loveseat. When the quietness finally sets in, a niggling urge to pick up my phone and dial Ivy's number eats at me. It's later now, after ten, and I expect she's up and going for her morning jog.

I want to open up to her, tell her why I've been so closed off and cold. I want to take the risk and hope she'll be there for me through this. As much as I want to make her mine, I know I don't deserve her.

CHAPTER FOURTEEN

IVY

After how Brix reacted to me being gone, I'm concerned when he doesn't come home for the last two nights. They even canceled their show at Vibrate on Friday.

No one knew the details why. The notice posted on their Facebook page said, "due to a family emergency." Kyla said Madden wouldn't give her any details, only that it had something to do with Brix's mom, and he couldn't be there.

I'm sitting on the couch in the living room, getting ready to paint my toes when he comes stalking through the front door. His black baseball cap is pulled down low, covering his face. He's dressed in a pair of black gym shorts, something I rarely see him wearing, and a cut-off muscle shirt. Brix always looks handsome, but right now he looks exhausted with dark circles under his eyes, like he hasn't slept in days.

"Brix," I murmur, setting the bottle of polish down on the coffee table. "Where have you been?"

He reaches into his pocket, tossing his keys on the counter as he shoulders past me.

"Aren't you going to talk to me?"

"I don't feel like talking right now. Soon, just not right now."

"Is everything okay?" I ask, jogging up the steps behind him.

"I said I don't want to talk about it."

"Okay, well, can you at least look at me?"

He ignores me, pushing the door to his bedroom open, sauntering toward his dresser to pull out a pair of boxer briefs and shorts, tossing them on his bed. He walks past me, stepping in front of his closet in search of a shirt before adding it to the pile.

Crossing my arms in front of me, I stare at his back, debating if I want to give up and walk out of here. After what happened between us the other night, then lying in bed missing him for the past two nights, I hadn't expected he'd go back to treating me this way.

Well, I guess I should say I hoped we hadn't gone back to this.

He flings his hat on top of his dresser, ignoring me like I'm not even standing here. With his back facing me, he peels his shirt off. The Roman lettering with "Ward" printed in ink spans his upper back.

His hair is pulled back, matted to his head.

Even though he doesn't look like his usual self, he looks incredibly sexy. Standing in front of me, without a shred of emotion, he grabs the waistband of his shorts and drops them to the floor with his shirt, leaving him naked.

"What are you doing?"

"What does it look like I'm doing?"

I can't help myself, I let my eyes eat up every inch of his body. The arrogant asshole he is, he doesn't even try to cover. He stands there, letting me drink him in like I'm dehydrated and only his body can fill me with all the nourishment I need.

When my eyes finally fall on his, I'm relieved to find something more than exhaustion on his face. Judging by the size of his, uh, package, I can tell he enjoys it just as much as I do.

"Well, now I guess I'm going to have to do something about this, too." His hand wraps around his length, he reaches for his clothes before waltzing through the door.

It takes a second for my feet to catch up with him, my mind in other places thinking about his hand on himself again. After the first time of watching him in the shower, I'm eager at the thought of getting a second viewing when I see him head toward the bathroom.

He disappears through the door, only this time he shuts it behind him. The sound of the lock clicking feels like a punch in the gut.

I hate that he's pushing me away and how easily I find myself back in this place, disliking how he makes me feel embarrassed and rejected.

I dejectedly walk back down the stairs and collapse on the couch, continuing to paint my toenails. I don't have long before I have to get ready for my shift.

After his shower, Brix is dressed in his usual black Dickies. This time he's dressed in a white t-shirt and his all-black Vans. He mutters something about heading over to Tysin's to prep for their show tonight. They store their equipment and practice at his house. He doesn't say anything, he just grabs his keys off the counter and stalks out the door.

It's on my mind the entire time as I get ready and all along the drive to the bar. My eyes keep checking the back door, waiting for when he and the guys come through to set up.

The knot in my stomach starts to lessen some when he arrives, and I see his eyes search the bar looking for me. I can't be sure since he's on the opposite side of the room, but for a second, I think he smiles when he finds me looking back at him, too.

Whatever happened, whatever is going on with him, something tells me it has nothing to do with us. As much as I want to push him, just like he's done to me, I know I need to give him time and space to work through whatever it is.

After they arrive, time seems to fly by. Every chance I get, my eyes seem to drift back to the stage, watching them set up for their show. Once they finish, the guys head toward the bar in search of drinks. It's the same moment Trevor shows up, taking a seat at the same barstool he used the first night we met, near where I'm working.

"Hey, Trev," I say, smiling. He looks good, his hair curling on the ends, giving him a more boyish look.

I can't help but think back to the nickname Brix gave him, feeling guilty comparing the similarities between the two. Despite Brix's disapproval, Trevor has been nothing but good to me. He's tried reaching out a couple of times over the past few days. All his attempts were met with no response.

He doesn't deserve for me to ignore him. The fact he's even sitting here in front of me, talking to me, says far more about the kind of man he is.

"Hey, Ivy." He grins. Reaching into the cooler beneath the bar, I grab him a tallboy of Busch Light. Popping the tab, I set it down in front of him.

"Thanks." He flashes me a wink, as Brix takes a seat next to him.

Trevor glances between the two of us, uncertain of how I'll react after the last two incidents.

"Hey, man, I think I saw you outside our house the other day," Brix says, ignoring the fact he saw us together at the fair and on the boardwalk. He looks serious, but I know better than to believe he's being nice. "What's your name again? Frank, right?"

I bite down on my lower lip, my eyes widen at the thought of what's about to come out of his mouth next, glancing from Trevor back to me. Goddammit, I want to smack him upside the head right now.

"Ahhh, nah, man. It's Trevor."

"Right, Trevor. I must've confused you with someone else then."

I glare at Brix, reaching to grab him a bottle of beer, sliding it across the counter to him. I don't even bother opening it for him. He grins, knowingly, flashing me a wink that says not to worry, opening the top and tossing the cap at me. Catching it with my hand, I mouth back at him that he's a pain in my ass, which earns me a laugh.

I busy myself with serving beers to the other guys, as Trevor makes side conversation with Brix about their show tonight.

"So, I was wondering," Trevor says, when things start to slow down. Taking the towel from my back pocket, I wipe down the top of the bar, waiting for what he's about to say.

"If you don't have any plans tomorrow night, I was hoping you'd want to go out again?"

God, I hate to do this right now. I can feel the heat from Brix's eyes blazing into the side of my face, knowing he's listening, despite him trying to pretend he's talking to the guys.

"Actually, I've been meaning to talk to you about that."

"Really?"

"Umm, yeah," I murmur, biting down on my lip again. Peering up under my eyelashes, I look at Trevor, and it seems he realizes our conversation isn't moving in the direction he had been hoping for.

He reaches for his beer, taking a swig before he sets the can down on the counter as if trying to prepare for what I'm about to say next.

"I'm not going to be staying here in Carolina Beach much longer. I, uh, am only here for the summer, you know. I'm not looking for anything serious. It'll only be a few more weeks before I head back to school."

"Right, of course. I get you." He nods, taking another drink of his beer before flashing me a forced smile.

After my night with Brix, I know the spark I feel with him is incomparable to what I feel with Trevor, and it's for the best that we go our separate ways. He's a great guy and he deserves someone who wants the same thing he does.

I leave him alone while he finishes his beer. He doesn't say anything more as he sets a twenty on the counter. He flashes me a brief wave when I catch him walking out.

"You broke his dead heart." Brix chuckles.

"You really are a jackass, you know that?"

"I'm beginning to think it's one of your favorite things about me."

Tossing my head back, I scoff. "You're out of your damn mind."

His eyes bore into me, watching my reaction to him, feeling the heat in his stare. "What time you off tonight?"

"Midnight. Why?"

He nods. "Wait for me, will ya? Don't leave when you're off."

"Okayyy..." I draw out. "What are we doing?"

"You'll see."

He chuckles again when I stare out the corner of my eye at him, untrusting.

"I promise, I'm not going to hurt you or anything."

"That doesn't make me feel better about this."

"I said, I promise." He winks as he finishes off his beer. He throws a fifty down on the bar, and without a word, takes off toward the other end of the bar with the guys.

My mind is preoccupied with what Brix has in store for us later while running through all the possible explanations for why he'd want me to wait for him. I keep going back to what Kyla said about him canceling his show last night and his family emergency.

I had been worried when he was gone, so I had called my mom, checking on her and Jasper while on their trip to Aruba. I didn't want to cause them to worry unnecessarily either but hinted at whether Jasper had spoken to Brix at all while he was away.

Nothing.

Whatever it is, I reassure myself he'll tell me when he's ready. For now, I'm going to focus on the next few weeks we have left together before I head back to school.

'Cause when I do, not only will I be saying goodbye to him, I'm saying goodbye to whatever this is between us. As fun as it may be, it'll be for the best.

CHAPTER FIFTEEN

IVY

All night, no matter what I was doing or how busy it was, my eyes kept finding their way back to the back of the bar.

Back to Brix.

A few times throughout the night, I found myself singing along to the lyrics. When Brix got to the part where he encourages the crowd to take a drink with him, I couldn't help but smile at the grin on his face when he caught me joining in.

He's dressed looking fine as hell in his A Rebels Havoc band t-shirt, his hat pulled on backward. Something about his hat with his dark smoldering eyes, watching him tug his lip ring into his mouth, makes me want to pull him into the back room and push him against the wall.

It is after midnight when they wrap up their show. Jayde recently hired a couple of new girls, so I am able to get off right as they are done playing. The crowd usually disappears around that time anyway.

Kyla is here, so I swing by her table to chat with her while I wait for Brix to finish packing up for the night. Spotting him weave his way through the crowd of people, a tinge of jealousy washes through me seeing women reaching for him, rubbing over his chest or trying to talk to him. He doesn't bother to stop and talk to them, his eyes transfixed on mine, stalking toward me like he has only one thing on his mind, and that's getting to me.

"You ready?" he asks when he finally makes his way to me.

Kyla's eyes blaze into us, not used to seeing us interact like this.

"Yeah," I say, swiping my purse from the back of my chair as I stand.

"I'm sorry." Kyla pauses, holding her hands between us. "Where are you two going?"

I wait for Brix to respond, not quite sure how to answer her.

"Out."

"Out." I shrug, smiling.

He doesn't say another word. Not caring who sees us or what they may think, he grabs my hand and leads me away from Kyla. Giggling, I glance over my shoulder seeing Kyla's mouth fall open, flashing a tentative smile as I wave goodbye.

"Okay, seriously, are you going to tell me now? Where are we going?"

Our fingers wrap together while we move through the crowd toward the back door near the parking lot.

"For a drive. Will you stop asking me now?"

"You're not up to anything *bad*, are you?"

"Now *that* I can't promise you. I do promise I won't let anything bad happen to you. Is that better?"

Stepping into the cool night air, he drags his thumb along the back of my hand, leading me across the gravel parking lot to where his truck is parked.

I'm in love with Brix's truck. It reminds me of something my grandpa drove when I was younger. It's an older Chevy, all black with black rims, lowered to the ground. It's exactly what I would picture Brix driving, too.

He opens the door, and I let go of his hand, moving to climb in when he pulls me back, catching me off guard.

"I don't think so." He grins, pushing me up against the side of the truck, leaning in to kiss me.

When our lips connect, I slide my hand up his chest and wrap it around his neck, holding him to me. Not caring who could possibly see us, I give into the feel of his body pressed against me and the taste of his mouth on mine.

Our tongues tangle, his body rocking against mine. His hands holding my face, not shying away from taking what he wants.

When he pulls back, he brushes his mouth against my ear, whispering, "You taste so good, Ivy."

His words drip with desire, and I know he's not talking about right now. He's remembering our first night, and I can't help but remember the way he tasted then, too.

My hands grip his forearms, trying to hold myself steady.

"Get in before I change my mind and fuck you right here in this parking lot."

"Fuck," he mutters, when I let out a small moan, pausing to adjust himself before shutting the door behind me.

When he shoves the keys in the ignition and pulls out of his spot, I don't bother asking again where he's taking me, but it's clear he isn't going for an aimless drive. He has a destination in mind. With the cloud of desire still hanging over us, I sit back and enjoy the ride.

"It's a little too late for a swim, don't you think?" I mention when he turns the truck onto the road leading us down near Carolina Beach.

"Even if that's what we were doing, I wouldn't be looking to just swim anyway."

Picturing the two of us skinny dipping in the ocean has me folding my legs, desperately seeking some friction at the mere thought.

He pulls his truck up along the beach. The typical crowd filling the boardwalk is missing, leaving only the midnight sky twinkling overhead.

He puts the truck in park, leaving it on and adjusting the music to a playlist.

"I want to say I'm sorry for earlier. It's been a shitty few days. I'm guessing you're probably wondering where I was and why I didn't come home. I want you to know it's not what you probably think."

"I didn't know what to think, honestly."

"Well, I knew you had to have noticed I was gone when you woke up. I wanted to text you, but I didn't know what to say or how much to tell you. I had a lot of shit going on."

"You know you can talk to me, right? Whatever it is, whatever you need. You can tell me."

He tilts his head back against the headrest, turning to face me. His eyes fall on my lips, staring at my mouth.

"It was my mom," he murmurs. I don't bother to tell him I reached out to Kyla and asked her to talk to Madden. I don't push him to explain further. I give him the time to collect his thoughts and tell me whatever's on his mind.

"She has an alcohol problem, has for years. The last time this happened, she had passed out in her car outside the bar when the owner found her. She at least had half a mind not to drive home. She decided to sleep it off in the front seat of her piece of shit car. That was probably the worst I've ever seen her." He pauses, staring out through the windshield, lost in thought.

"Anyway, this wasn't the first time something like this has happened. She's woken up in places and not remembered how she got there or even where her car was. I picked her up that day and immediately took her to the hospital. I was fed up, ya know? I told her she needed to be admitted, it was time for her to get some help."

"I'm sure it wasn't easy for you, but it's what she needed."

"Well, I wish I could say it helped. When she got out, she was mad. She didn't stay sober for long. She pushed me away and stopped talking to me. My uncle Travis called, told me he found her passed out again. This time I was going to help her through her detox, and when she was done, I was giving her a choice. She either got the help she needed, once and for all, or I was walking away."

"I'm sorry, Brix."

Unbuckling the seat belt, I slide across the seat closer to him. There's not much room for us, but he welcomes me, pulling my legs over his, draping them over his lap.

Silence fills the space around us, as he runs his hand up my thigh.

"Your skin is so soft," he says, changing the subject.

He stares up at me under his dark eyelashes.

Covering my hand with his, he continues, "Anyway, it took a lot of fighting and arguing with her. She was livid when she found out we went through her house and threw out all her alcohol. She had nothing left. She called me all sorts of names, told me I was a piece of shit, but in the end, she agreed."

He squeezed his eyes shut, tipping his head back against the headrest once again.

"I can't believe she'd say that to you."

"She's not wrong, though."

"What?" I grab his chin in my hand, forcing him to face me.

"C'mon, Ivy. Be honest. I'm a fuckin' prick. I do and say shit without even caring about the consequences or how it hurts people. Look at how I've treated you. For years, YEARS, I've treated you like garbage. Don't sit here and tell me I'm wrong when we both know that's a load of bullshit."

"You're right."

Holding his hand out, as if saying "thank you" for agreeing with him.

"You do and say things without thinking it through, but it doesn't make you a bad person."

"How can you say or believe that, Ivy? How can you even sit here with me right now? I don't even get it."

"Brix, tell me why. Why did you treat me the way you did?"

"I told you..." he starts, but I cut him off.

"No, I don't want to hear some bullshit response about you being a piece of shit or calling yourself a prick. Tell me the truth. Why did you treat me that way?"

"You want to know the honest to God truth?"

"Of course, I do."

"Do you remember the day I saw you in the hallway outside Principal Taylor's office?"

My eyes narrow, not remembering what he's talking about. He picks up on my confusion and continues, filling in the blanks.

"I had stormed out of his office. I was upset, shoving shit from my locker into my bag, ready to leave school, when you approached me. You didn't have a clue what you had walked into, but you stopped anyway and asked if I was okay."

The dots start to connect. He had been swearing under his breath, tears filling his eyes when I stopped him and asked if he was alright.

"My parents had separated three months before. My mom, who always had a problem with drinking, started to get worse when my father filed for divorce. He said it was for 'irreconcilable differences,' but what he really meant was my mom is a drunk, and he had turned to getting his rocks off with his assistant."

"Oh, God." I cover my mouth.

I knew Brix was pissed at his dad for getting married again after his comment about getting a prenup. Of course, he would want his parents to be together, but his anger makes more sense now.

He looks down, his arm sitting on top of my knee with his hand clenched around the bottom of the steering wheel.

"I'm sorry, Ivy, I don't think it's going to last with them either. This is who he is. He gets bored in one relationship and finds his way onto the next one. He couldn't be monogamous to save his life."

He scoffs, rolling his eyes as it turns from a laugh to a growl, clearly annoyed talking about it.

"Anyway, the day outside the principal's office, you saw me walking out. I was pissed off to the point I was damn near tears. I had seen you around, but up until that point, we hadn't spoken. Of course, I noticed you, I mean, fuck, how could I not?"

The way he said it, I'm surprised. What does he mean he noticed me? He sounds frustrated at the admission, but not in the same way it was talking about his dad's promiscuity.

"Brix," I whisper, reaching for his chin once again, turning him to look at me. "What does that mean?"

"It means every time I saw you, I thought about how beautiful you looked. How kind you always had been to everyone around you. You were shy, that much was certain. You kept to yourself, but that day, you weren't. You stopped at my locker, seeing I was upset, and you asked me if I was okay. Fuck, Ivy. I was so fucking mean. I remember the look on your face, the shock hit your eyes. I felt like the biggest asshole in the world, but it was like I felt the need to warn you. To convince you there was nothing good in me that deserved you or your kindness. So, I pushed you away in the only way I knew how. I took my hurt and threw it back at you, thinking it would somehow help me feel better about my shitty life."

Tears fill the brim of my eyes, pressing my lips into a firm line, I try to hold it all together.

He's right. He was a jerk, and I never quite understood why. I tried to stay away from him after that day, but it was like life had its way of throwing us back together.

"You didn't deserve it, Ivy. Not one bit, just like I don't deserve to be sitting here with you now."

I reach my hand out for his. It's still fixed around the bottom of the steering wheel, white-knuckled against the leather. His forearm flexes and I trace my fingers over every ridge lining his muscles. As soon as my fingers find his, he releases his hold turning his hand over, wrapping his fingers in mine. I can't help but feel like he's releasing everything he's held back from me, giving into me now.

"I forgive you," I murmur, leaning to rest my head on his shoulder.

"I don't deserve your forgiveness, but like the asshole I am, I'm going to take it. I'm going to take you and hold onto you. I don't want to let you go."

CHAPTER SIXTEEN

BRIX

Pulling in front of the house, I spot Ivy's car parked in the driveway, relieved to see she's home. All afternoon at band practice, I couldn't get her off my mind.

On my way back, I got this idea to take her out on a date, which is something I've never done. Sure, I've hung out with women but not with the same intentions as I have with Ivy.

After the night down by the beach, things have begun to shift between us. A part of me wants to hit stop, pull out and run, but I don't.

Walking through the door, I search for any sign of her in the kitchen or dining room. I'm about to yell her name up the stairs when I step into the living room to find her curled up on the couch with a blanket pulled over her.

It wasn't long ago she found me passed out in the same place. To think how much has changed since that day compared to where we are now.

Our parents are still gone on their honeymoon. They're supposed to fly in tomorrow afternoon, which means it's our last night alone without them dropping in for God knows how long.

Kneeling next to her, I lean in to press a kiss against her lips. Her scent engulfs me, her hair smelling like strawberries mixed with something uniquely Ivy.

For a second, I consider waking her up in some bullshit romantic way, like kissing her on her lips and whispering something like, "wake up beautiful."

She chooses that moment to roll over onto her back, moving the blanket off her in the process. Her tank top is pulled up, exposing her tan stomach. Her shorts are rolled at the waist, making them even shorter than they already are. Her leg is bent, and all I can think about is how likely I'd be able to peel them off and taste her again without waking her right away.

Running my hand over her stomach, my eyes bounce from her face to where my hand is moving down toward her hip to the apex of her thigh. She moans slightly, and I pause, waiting for her to open her eyes and catch me. When she stops, I continue my way down, reaching the edge of her shorts. I feel her heat through the cotton of her shorts, and I bite my lip to stop myself from moaning, gliding my finger along her inner thigh up toward her pussy.

It doesn't take me long to discover she's not wearing any panties. The urge to wake her, bend her over my lap, and smack her ass consumes me until my finger slides over her folds into her warm, wet pussy.

"Motherfucker," I mutter, tracing my finger along her opening.

She moans again, widening her legs more. "Actually, wouldn't that make me a brother fucker?"

"Get your ass up, now."

She grins, adjusting her shirt when she moves to sit up. "Don't even dare," I murmur, stopping her from pulling it back down, "in fact, take that shit off. Now."

This time, the words are much more pointed. Stern.

"Yes, sir." She giggles, standing in front of me while I recline back on the couch, watching her.

I'm not even surprised when I find not only is she not wearing underwear, she's also without a bra, too. She looks like a fucking dream.

Her breasts jiggle as she pulls the top over her head, tossing the shirt back at me, hitting me in the face.

I'm unamused, reaching to pull the shirt away to find her with her hands on her hips, grabbing for the waistband of her pants, waiting for further instruction.

I motion with my finger to drop them, too. She licks her lips, excitement lighting her face when she slides them down her legs. I'm starting to wonder if she planned this shit when she props her leg on the cushion next to me, teasing me with her pussy.

"Now what, sir."

"Turn," I command. She bites down on her lip but does as I say, turning until her back faces me.

Her ass, fuck me, that ass looks so fucking good. I'm starting to run through all the ways I could take her right here and now when she does something that takes me by utter surprise.

Bending over, she presses her hands against the oak coffee table and spreads her legs open for me. She glances over her shoulder, a devilish grin lining her mouth.

I don't even hesitate as I scoot close to her, reaching out to grab her ass cheek in my hand, spreading them before smacking her skin. The loud slap echoes around the room as she pushes her ass back toward me.

With both hands gripping her ass, I lean forward and trace the tip of my tongue from her clit all the way up to her hole.

"Holyyyy fuck," she groans.

Dipping my tongue into her pussy, I fuck her like it's the last thing I'll ever do. She tosses her head back, her long, brown hair fanning over her while I hold her against me. My tongue alternates between fucking her to flicking over her clit. With each stroke, she grinds against me, seeking more, wanting more.

Pulling back, I run my finger along her folds, mimicking the same motion before entering her. I give her exactly what she wants, her body rocking against me, her breathy moans filling my ears, urging me on.

I'm so turned on, I'm damn near busting through my fucking shorts. Falling back, my hands are on my zipper, making quick work of pulling down my pants.

"Get the fuck over here. Now."

She smiles, her cheeks rosy, clearly enjoying being told what to do. Wrapping my hand around the base of my cock, I hold my dick out for her as she kneels on the floor in front of me.

She's obviously not worried about my piercing anymore when the tip of my dick hits the back of her throat. My fingers tangle in her hair as she moves back down, gagging when she takes me deep.

"Fuck, baby."

She moans with every thrust; her hand moves over me, covering my own.

"C'mere," I growl, as she moves to climb on top of me.

Reaching up, I grab her breast in my hand, taking her nipple and sucking it into my mouth while I squeeze the other. Releasing it with a pop, she positions herself above me before sinking down, taking all of me until she's pressed to the hilt.

"God damn. You feel so fucking good."

My fingers dig into her hips as her arm snakes around my neck. I continue my assault on her nipple while she works her pussy over me. With each slow ascend, she follows it through with a fast and deep descend until I'm panting with how much I want her. She rotates her hips, driving me fucking wild with need.

"Dear God, Ivy, the things I dream of doing to you would make the devil blush."

Her movements turn urgent, and I do my best to hold on. Slipping my thumb down between us, I brush my finger over her clit, watching as she tosses her head back. Feeling her pussy clench around me brings me to the edge.

"More, more, more," she chants over me. Pressing my thumb down, I change my movements to throw her off, and her body starts to tremble. I'm so far gone at this point.

She collapses against me, her arms wrapping around my neck, while the aftershocks rake through her body. When she's finished, her body melts into mine. Goose bumps spread out over her skin, so I reach out for her blanket and pull it over us.

"You like to act like this sweet side of you is new and foreign, but you're pretty good at it, ya know?"

"Only with you."

She pulls back, her hand against my cheek as she presses a soft kiss on my lips, and I let her. I'm in over my head now. I'd give her anything she wants at this point.

"Speaking of romantic shit, I was going to ask if you wanted to go out tonight."

"Like a date?" She grins.

"Yeah, sure."

"Sure?"

"I mean, yes."

She laughs. "Who would've thought, Brix Ward, asking me out on a date?"

"You want me to smack your ass again?"

"Maybe." She smiles, rotating her hips to push her ass further into my hands.

"You're not helping right now." The movement causes her pussy to rub against me again.

She leans away from me, holding her hand up, feigning innocence.

"I'm sorry, am I the one doing something wrong here?" Just as she says the word "wrong," she rocks back over me. Reaching out, I grab her breast in my hand, pinching her nipple as desire glosses over her eyes.

"Brix," she moans, continuing to rock again.

"If you continue to fuck with me, we're not going anywhere, Ivy."

"This is our last night home together," she whispers. "You don't have to take me out. I'd prefer to stay here and watch a movie anyway. We can even pick something scary, and I'll pretend to be afraid so you can hold me."

"Is that what you want?"

She nods. I realize then she really did plan for this to happen. Dressed in nothing but her t-shirt and shorts, she knew when I walked through the door and saw her sprawled out, I wouldn't be able to resist touching her.

"How about we do both? We go out for a little bit, then we come back here, and I fuck you until you're so worn out, you'll want to sleep for the next three days straight."

Her fingers wrap around the base of my neck, nails raking through my hair. She gets this distant look in her eyes before she gives in.

"As long as I get to fall asleep next to you tonight, I don't care where we are or what we do."

An emotion passes over her eyes that wasn't there a moment before. She takes a deep breath, before I press another kiss against her soft lips. What was once full of urgent need is now replaced with a slow passion. She holds my face in her hands, deepening the kiss.

When she pulls back, she flashes me a small smile before she moves to stand. My eyes track her body, watching her bend down to pick up her t-shirt. A low growl escapes me when she tosses a look over her shoulder, grinning back at me.

"You wanted to go out."

"Like I said, you're still not helping."

"My apologies, sir." I watch her saunter toward the stairs, swiping her shorts off the floor in the process. I soak in the sight of her sexy ass and those legs as she walks away from me. When I reach down to adjust myself, she clears her throat, drawing my attention back to her.

"Get ready for our date, Brix, because when we get back home, you're mine."

CHAPTER SEVENTEEN

BRIX

"Game On, really? What are we doing?" Ivy questions, glancing out through the windshield up at the sign.

"What? You scared you're gonna lose?"

She raises her eyebrow, taunting me before she laughs, jumping out of my truck, not bothering to wait for me.

"Whatever it is, Brix, you're going down."

I laugh, staring at her ass as she does, watching her walk through the front door.

Once we're inside, I hold two fingers up for the guy standing at the front counter.

"Two for laser tag, please."

"You got it." He turns to grab the laser guns and vests from a row of tactical gear hanging on the wall.

"You really have no idea what you're getting yourself into, do you?" She perches her hip against the counter, crossing her arms in front of her.

Grabbing her waist, I step into her and tilt my head in near her neck. "Trust me, baby. I think I have an idea. I'm just looking forward to seeing you all riled up."

"Uh-huh." She snickers, pushing back at my chest.

I hand the guy cash, paying for our bill, while Ivy pulls on a vest as I follow suit. I can't deny how hard my dick gets seeing her strapped in. She pulls her hair up away from her face like she's preparing for battle.

The guy at the counter points the trigger at the front of each of our vests, activating the sensors.

"Alright, you have twenty minutes. The mission is to find the medallions hidden throughout the course. The first person to collect all three without being shot three times wins. Yours will be red," he says, pointing to me, "and yours will be green."

"Wait, will we have a chance to get in there and get a feel for it before it starts?" she asks.

"Get a feel for it? What do you think this is?"

"I'm just saying, I don't want you right on my ass when I walk through the door. I want time to get away from you before it starts."

"Yes, you'll get fifteen seconds once the door shuts before the timer starts."

"Okay, good. Got it." She rotates her shoulders before she widens her legs, crouching down to stretch.

I just stand and stare at her, taking in the way her leg muscles flex with each move. I don't doubt the teenage fucker behind the counter is doing the same, but I don't bother to tell him to keep his eyes off her.

I'll let him get a show, give him an idea of the kind of woman he has to look forward to when he's older. Ivy's body is a fucking ten.

"Baby, you want to turn around and do that for me?" I whisper, quiet enough for only her to hear.

"Not gonna happen, Ward."

"We haven't even started yet. Can't you give me a little taste?"

"Nope." She glares at me. The moment the vest went on, she turned serious.

"Alright, you're ready to go."

Ivy nods, leading the way through the door and into the laser tag course. It's dark. Green lights pepper the walls pointing toward the floor.

"Don't follow me, Ward!" Ivy shouts over her shoulder, jogging away from me. I take off, deciding to head in the opposite direction.

A robotic voice plays through the speakers, counting down from five until it announces "BEGIN," as all the lights flash.

Pressing my back against the wall, I hold my gun out in front of me, quiet with every step I make, surveying my surroundings, searching for any sign of my red medallions or Ivy.

A flicker of movement catches the corner of my eye. Ivy jogs past me, and I cut across toward her. Leaning my shoulder against the wall, I hold the gun up near my face, careful as I turn the corner.

I am met by Ivy's smiling face with her gun pointed right at my chest, firing.

"Gotcha." She giggles, taking off running again. It takes a few seconds before my gun unlocks, so I take off behind her.

"You're gonna pay for that!" I shout, as I hear the signal ring out, alerting she found one of her medallions.

"Fuck," I gripe. I stop in my tracks, pulling back in search of mine. I need to catch up to her, and she's already ahead of me.

The next fifteen minutes is spent running through the course as I quickly track down two of my medallions before I run into Ivy again. This time, I'm the victor and shoot her first.

"Damn you, Ward." She laughs before she takes off running again.

I love how into this she is. Ivy's the kind of girl who will chill with you watching college football on a Saturday, but then be down to go out with you and a few of your buddies at night.

It's what I love about her.

I hear the signal announcing Ivy found her second medallion. Now we're tied, and whoever finds their last one is the winner.

I dash toward the last corner. It's the only corner of the room I haven't staked out yet, so I'm willing to bet it's there. Carefully keeping an eye out for any sign of Ivy, I push my back against the wall and sidestep along the exterior of the room.

I spot my medallion in the far corner and quickly take off toward it, thwarted when I come face-to-face with

Ivy when I do. Pointing her laser at me, she shoots and earns her second kill before heading off to snatch her last medallion.

"Hell yeah," she cheers, jumping up and down. Dropping the gun at my side, I stalk her down, pushing her against the wall. She shrieks in surprise.

Sweat dots her brow; hair pulled back in a ponytail.

"You're so fucking sexy, you know that?"

I lift her by her thighs and hold her body against mine, attacking her neck. Her arms wrap around me, holding on while I grind into her.

"Brix, we probably shouldn't..." She breathes out slowly. "We probably shouldn't do this here."

"The fuck we shouldn't. I'll take you when and where I want to."

"Oh, God," she moans, tilting her head back giving me better access to her. She doesn't need to know I may have slipped him a twenty for a few extra minutes in here alone.

I guess you can say I had a feeling I was going to want her by the time we were done.

Pulling back from her neck, her mouth crashes down on mine, our tongues tangle together, my dick grinding against her heat. I've never been more turned on from kissing someone as I am with her.

Her hands frame my face, nails digging into the skin of my scalp.

Lowering her to her feet, I turn her, so her back is pressed against my chest. She pushes her ass out toward me, rubbing the curve against my aching cock.

"You're trying to kill me right now, aren't you?"

She moans in response, loud enough for me to hear over the sound of Shinedown blaring through the speakers.

My fingers find the button of her shorts, popping them open as I slide my hand into the front, desperately seeking her warmth.

"Good girl," I whisper into her ear when I find she's still not wearing any panties.

"Brix." She moans my name, pushing her pussy into my hand.

I sink my finger further into her wet heat, first one finger before adding another. Twisting my other hand into her hair, I pull her head back until it's resting on my shoulder, leaving kisses along her neck down to her shoulder.

"That feel good, baby?"

She nods subtly. "I want to hear your words," I command.

"Ye-yes. So fucking good."

"Mm."

The palm of my hand pressed against her clit gives enough friction as she rides out her orgasm. Her pussy spasms around me while I nip at the skin along her neck.

Her arm reaches up, pulling me in to kiss her. Holding my fingers out in front of her, I nod my head for her to open her mouth as she holds my hand in hers, dragging my fingers over her tongue.

If I wasn't damn near coming in my pants before, feeling my fingers in the back of her throat has me on the brink.

"If you keep that shit up, I'm going to pull your pants down and fuck you right here."

Ivy's eyes connect with mine. The look in her stare is tempting me to do it, not caring who could see us. I've done my best to shield her from prying eyes, but I can't promise no one would see us if that were to happen.

My phone vibrates in my pocket, I slip it out and check the screen. I don't recognize the number right away; it takes a second for me to realize it's likely someone from Newhaven.

"I gotta take this." Stepping back away from Ivy.

"Hello?"

"Yes, hi. Is this Brix Ward?"

"Yes."

"Hi, I'm Clint from Newhaven. I'm the director here, we spoke earlier this week about your mother."

"Yes, I remember."

"I'm sorry if I caught you at a bad time."

I realize then how bad this may sound, calling me later at night on Saturday with the sound of music blaring behind me.

"Yes, sorry. I'm out playing laser tag with a friend. Give me a moment to get somewhere quieter."

I mouth to Ivy, "It's about my mom." Unbuckling my vest, Ivy grabs it from me, urging me to go take the call as I jog toward the exit in search of somewhere private to talk.

"Sorry about that. Is everything okay? Is she alright?"

"Yes. I just wanted to call you about an incident that happened today. She walked out; said she wasn't going to commit to the program. Like we said when you brought her here, she's an adult, and there's nothing we can legally do to keep her here if she chooses to leave. She took off around one o'clock this afternoon and came back shortly after dinner time. It was clear she had been drinking when she was dropped off, but the good news is she came back."

Despite being frustrated she left, I'm relieved she made the choice to return, even though she had been drinking.

"We have her here. The next few hours will be hard for her as she battles with the urge to keep drinking. She has a dependency on alcohol, so it's almost like her body needs it to function or she feels crummy, but we'll help her through that process. I just wanted to reach out to you, so you were aware. She's here though, she's okay."

"Okay," I sigh, trying to process everything he just said. In the end, I focus on the fact she's back there. Travis and I both said we wanted her to choose this or it wasn't ever going to be effective.

"Thank you for giving me a call." I massage my fingers into my forehead as Ivy joins me, running her hand over my back, easing the tension I feel rising up in my body.

"Everything okay?" Ivy asks when I press the end button.

Sliding my phone back in my pocket, I take a deep breath wrapping my hand around her neck, pulling her into me and kissing her softly. Her hand grips my wrist, holding onto me when I tilt my head back.

"It's not right now, but it will be."

CHAPTER EIGHTEEN

IVY

I'm standing in the bathroom, putting the finishing touches on my makeup while talking to Kyla on speakerphone, when I hear Brix traipse through the front door.

She had just finished telling me about how Tysin was waiting beside her car when she got off work. Once I hear him, making an entrance like he always does, my mind zones out on everything she's saying.

"Get your sweet ass down here!" Brix shouts.

By the long pause on the other end of the line, I'm guessing she heard him, too.

"Was that Brix?" Kyla asks, in the middle of her sentence.

Shuffling my stuff back in my makeup bag, I swipe my phone off the counter, shoving everything in the linen closet. Stepping out of the bathroom, he mutters something about smacking my ass when he stops in his tracks, eyes falling on the phone in my hand.

"Yeah, it was." My eyes widen, trying to signal him to zip it.

I haven't quite made it to telling Kyla about what's been going on with the two of us. I guess in my mind, I'm still waiting for the moment things inevitably change. For the other shoe to drop, so to speak.

"What's going on? Is everything okay?"

I mouth Kyla's name, pointing to my phone. He doesn't seem to give a shit, cornering me against the wall, sliding his arms around me, kissing my neck.

My body trembles, reacting to the feel of his hands and lips on my skin.

"Uh, yeah," I stammer. "Everything's great. Just perfect."

I playfully push away from him, and he stumbles back. The look in his eyes shifts, as he quirks his eyebrow up challenging. He stalks after me into my bedroom.

"I just realized what time it is, and I need to head out to Whiskey Barrel," I lie. The words sound all wrong.

"Right…" She trails off, chuckling, not believing me. I quickly leave her with promises of calling her tomorrow to make plans to stop by one night this week.

"I need to know more about that thing you were telling me about earlier."

She giggles. "You two have fun."

As soon as I hang up and toss my phone on the bed, I peek over my shoulder to Brix, who's leaning against the desk at the opposite end of my room.

His arms are crossed in front of his chest, brushing the pad of his thumb over his bottom lip, tracking my every move.

He's dressed in his usual black t-shirt and jeans. Probably the only person in North Carolina who still wears them in the middle of summer, but that's Brix for ya. His dark eyes follow me as I saunter over to my closet, searching for something to wear.

"I thought you had band practice?"

"I did. I wanted to see you before you went to work."

Things between us have begun to shift. Conversations that used to be clipped, full of smartass comments tossed back and forth at each other, are different. He says things that were so unlike him before but now wrap themselves around my heart.

I give him a small smile, and he eyes me like he doesn't know why or what he's done to earn it. He hesitates for a moment before pushing off the desk to approach me. I turn back to my closet, searching for something to wear as he comes up behind me, snaking his arms around my waist.

"You smell so fucking delicious," Brix moans while tracing his nose over the column of my neck. His hands slip beneath the cotton of my tank, trailing a line across my shorts.

"How much longer until you have to be at work?"

Both of our eyes turn to the time displayed on the alarm clock sitting atop my nightstand. "I still have about fifteen minutes until I need to leave if I want to make it on time."

"Not enough time for all I want to do to you, but plenty of time if we focus on the important parts." His teeth drag along my tender skin as a soft growl leaves his throat.

Leaning back against his shoulder, I relish the feel of his hands on me.

"I wish I didn't have to work tonight so I could stay home with you," I whisper.

He nods in agreement as I turn to wrap my arms around his neck.

"Why don't you come with me? I can serve you drinks, and you can hang out while I'm working."

It's a Thursday night, so I don't expect it to be busy with our normal weekend crowd. When he doesn't answer me right away, my guard goes up sensing his reluctance.

When we're here, we don't have to think about our parents or the consequences which would come with us being together. All of that changes when we leave the house and people we know are around, eyes are on us, questions are being asked. We haven't even figured out how to sort through what to say. Well, maybe I haven't figured it out. Brix just would refuse to answer, not bothering in the least what anyone thinks.

"Never mind. It's fine, forget I asked. I'll be home around midnight if you want to wait up for me?"

I try to push the look in his eyes out of my mind, turning back to my closet, swallowing down the ball of emotion forming in my throat. It shouldn't bother me this much.

"Whoa, whoa. What was that about?"

He reaches for my wrist, pulling me back to face him. I blink through the tears forming along the brim of my eyes. I hate how I'm letting this get to me.

His eyes search mine, pressing his hand against the side of my face to look at him.

"Whatever thoughts you had in your mind just now, push that shit out. It's not what you think it is. Of course, I want to come with you. I don't give a fuck about what anyone says, nor do I have any hesitations about us."

Wrapping my hand around his wrist, I lean into his palm when he presses a soft kiss against my mouth. I want to silence every doubt storming through my mind right now, forget every fear I've had, and enjoy having Brix here with me.

Deepening the kiss, I open my mouth to him, brushing my tongue across his lip, biting down on his lip ring. He growls, pulling me closer to him, so our chests are pressed firmly against each other.

"You drive me crazy," he whispers, breaking our kiss, his hand dragging over my hip down to squeeze my ass.

Grinning, I give him a quick kiss before backing up to finish getting ready.

He doesn't appear to like the answer, standing back, watching while I snag the top I was looking for from the hanger. Tossing the tank top over my head, he moans, watching me change in front of him while muttering something about forcing me to stay in.

He leaves me to run to his room, wanting to change his clothes after band practice, promising me he'll come with me and even agreeing to drive. When I protest, he assures me if he decides to take off, he'll come back and pick me up when I'm off work.

My shift is low key in comparison to my usual nights at Whiskey Barrel, but it flies by. Brix hangs out at the bar for most of the night, leaving for a bit when things pick up. It's after midnight when I punch out and walk outside, finding

Brix parked near the front. He's leaning against his tailgate looking mighty sexy with his arms and feet crossed in front of him.

The exhaustion setting in a moment ago is replaced with a spike of adrenaline when I see him push off his truck to approach me. Any reluctance I once feared is gone when I watch him stalk toward me with purpose, wrapping his hands on both sides of my face, leaning in to kiss me. Hard.

"Thank God you're off," he whispers, pulling back for a moment. "Do you know how hard it was not to kiss you when you were standing behind the bar? What is it about watching you work that drives me so fucking wild?"

Pulling me closer to him, he moans then slips his hand into mine, leading me over to the passenger side. He opens the door, waiting for me to climb in before he jogs around sliding in next to me.

Glancing over to where I'm sitting on the other end of the bench seat, his eyes dart between me and the empty space, then back to me. I'm damn near ready to crawl on top of him when he adjusts his hat backward, looking deliciously handsome.

Sliding across the seat closer to him, he turns on his truck, settling his hand on my inner thigh, holding me. The warmth in the pickup, combined with the darkness, brings back the fatigue I felt earlier as I lean my head against his shoulder.

We make small conversation about how the rest of my night went as he drives us back to our house. AC/DC plays on low as I peer up at him, mesmerized at the way his long eyelashes fan across the apples of his cheeks every time he blinks beneath the soft light of the streetlights shining above.

"How old were you when you got into singing?"

The question takes him by surprise as he looks down at me before adjusting his gaze back on the road. His hand finds its way back to mine, rubbing his thumb over my skin.

His eyes grow distant, he's lost in thought before he begins. "Around six or seven. I don't remember a lot from then, but I remember singing all the time. I was always the center of attention and loved performing. When I started to get older, and things with my parents weren't going well, and my mom was drinking heavily, I have memories of sitting with her when she was passed out or hungover, singing to her."

My heart aches thinking about a young Brix in those moments.

"I used it to distract me from what was going on around me. I started getting into it seriously when my parents were going through their divorce. The band, the guys, it was the only thing that helped. Without it, I don't know where I would be."

"I think this is what you were meant to be doing."

Lifting my hand to his mouth, he feathers a soft kiss against the back before relaxing it on his lap.

"How is she doing?"

He wavers again for a second before answering. I've noticed the emotion he carries around, seeing what his mom has been going through.

"She's doing good. I got to talk to her for a little bit yesterday, and she seemed happy. Better. She's becoming more and more of the mom I remember every day."

Pulling the car into the driveway, he sits back against the seat, his eyes finding mine in the dark moonlight. Running my hand along his jaw, I pull him closer to me, kissing his lips softly. His hand clenches my thigh as if he's holding on for dear life. When he leans his head back, breaking our connection, I see the emotion dancing in his eyes.

"I think you were meant to come into my life," he whispers, but the words hit me with impact. "I'm more myself with you than I've ever been."

Sliding my fingers in his, I kiss him with every ounce of love and passion I feel in me, but I can't find the words to say.

CHAPTER NINETEEN

IVY

My mom and Jasper haven't come around often despite flying home a week ago. Although the feeling around the house has shifted knowing any moment they could show up, nothing between Brix and me has changed.

If anything, our connection to each other only seems to grow more, regardless of feeling my guilt over what we are doing settling in more.

It's inevitable, our parents will find out about us eventually, but it makes me feel better every time Brix assures me it isn't going to change anything. Even on the nights when they stayed here instead of the loft, we still ended up sneaking into the other's bed.

I had grown accustomed to sleeping with Brix's strong arm banded around me every night. I wasn't sure what I was going to do when I went back to school and things shifted between us.

I hoped we would be able to make the long-distance thing work, but I also knew who Brix was. He had never been serious about anything in his life, except his music. The likelihood he'd continue to be interested in me when I was three hours away at school was something I thought about often.

In the end, I chose to push the fears out of my mind and enjoy what was left of the summer we had together.

The next couple of weeks flew by quickly. Between working at Whiskey Barrel and watching A Rebels Havoc play, we'd settled into a routine.

When my mom asked me out to lunch early in the week, I agreed with not an ounce of reluctance, knowing it wouldn't be long before I was saying goodbye to her, too. We decided to hit up the bar. They were known for their lunch menu. She hadn't seen where I had been working since moving back to town, so it was a perfect place to meet.

Sitting along the bench outside of the bar, I read through the text messages from Brix from earlier in the day when my mom's Audi pulls up and parks in the spot in front of me.

"Hi, sweetheart," she sings, pushing her door open and stepping out.

Her skin is tan, her dark brown hair curled and pulled back away from her face. She is beautiful in a Demi Moore sort of way.

"Hi, Momma." I stand, holding my arms out to her for a hug.

"I've missed you so much." Her stomach growls as she laughs, pressing her hand against her to cover up the sound. "Sorry, I guess my stomach wanted to say hi, too. I'm starving."

"Well, let's get something to eat." We laugh as I hold the door open for her to walk inside.

We pick out a booth along the outside wall. Jayde is the only person working the bar, the usual nighttime crowd gone, with only a few tables filled now.

Jayde stops by taking our order, as we fall into an easy conversation catching up. Although I've been staying with my mom for the past month and a half, we haven't really spent time together.

Her marriage to Jasper has been a whirlwind from the beginning, and all her time and attention have been wrapped up in him. Not that I blame her, it should be that way. It just hasn't left much time for us to connect with each other while I've been back.

"How was your trip to Aruba? You haven't really filled me in on how it went."

"Oh, Ivyana. It's beautiful there. Absolutely breathtaking. I've never seen anything like it. It was nice to get away, the two of us, away from work, and enjoy our time together. You know?"

"I bet! I saw some of the pictures you posted on Facebook."

She had shared snapshots of her and Jasper swimming near a waterfall. It was stunning, like something you'd see straight out of a magazine.

"I feel bad we haven't had a chance to do this yet since you've been back home. I've wanted to, you know. Things have been crazy." She pauses, taking a drink of her ice water.

"Yeah, I know. You've been busy, but it's okay."

"I'm sorry. You know that, right?"

"You don't have to be sorry, Mom. Seriously. There's nothing for you to be sorry for."

Growing up, my mom put all her time and attention into me. I knew she had dated, I heard her talking about it with her friends and my grandma from time to time, but she never brought anyone around. I asked her about it once, about why she hadn't been serious about anyone or why she hadn't remarried.

It's crazy to think about the conversation now. At the time, she told me she wasn't interested in being remarried. Her divorce from my father was hard on her. We never really talked about how or why it happened, but there were signs that whatever had led it to end had caused her to have a lot of distrust in relationships. She had closed herself off to the idea of being with anyone.

Thinking about that, knowing how my relationship with Brix could affect hers with Jasper, made me feel even more guilty. I didn't want what we had to cause any problems between them.

As selfish as it was for me, I also didn't want to stop what was growing between Brix and me.

"Things have changed so much, you know. Who would've thought a year ago, we'd be here? My relationship with Jasper moved so quickly. I never thought I'd get married again, but we wanted to make it work."

The way she says it, I can hear the tension in her voice. It is the first sign that whatever is going on, underneath the surface, it isn't all as it appears to be.

"It's good, though, right? You're happy?"

I hadn't intended for it to come out as a question, but she must've picked up on my apprehension as she lifts her glass to her mouth to take a drink. She flashes me a tense smile, eyes searching the bar for the answers that aren't coming to her.

"I'm very happy," she murmurs, pausing as if trying to gather her thoughts. "I just, you know, you have these pictures in your mind of how things are going to go. You're with someone, and you make these plans, you visualize what it will be like in your head. I knew Jasper was serious about his job. In fact, one of the things I love most about him is how hard he works. I had thought when we got married, he was going to take a step back, you know. We're getting older, our children are older. We talked about spending the summer down at the beach house and traveling together."

The sadness starts to creep in. I want to get up and hug her, find a way to ease the confusion and hurt she is feeling.

"I hadn't expected to spend most of my time in a loft or that he'd leave before eight every morning and come home after seven each night."

I understand her point. It doesn't seem like this is at all what they had talked about when they were planning out what their lives would be like.

"Have you tried talking to him about it?"

"I shouldn't be putting this on you, Ivyana. I'm sorry." She clasps her hands together.

"Mom, stop. You never talk to me about this stuff, but there's nothing wrong with telling me. Just answer me."

"I've tried." She presses her lips together in a firm line, forcing a smile. "You know, I should've known this was going to happen, and that's what I keep coming back to. He thought by showing his commitment to me, to each other, we'd be able to make it work."

My brows furrow in confusion. Is she suggesting they got married to fix their problems? That hardly sounds like the mom I know.

"I wanted to believe him, ya know? I love him."

"I know you do, Mom. I don't think that's the question here. It seems like you're the one who's doing all the sacrificing. What has he sacrificed for you?"

She nods her head in agreeance, leaning back against the booth seat as if all of her emotions sucked all the energy out of her. Jayde approaches then, setting down our plates.

Sitting in silence while we both eat, my mind drifts back to the night with Brix in the car when he mentioned he wasn't taking their marriage seriously. At the time, I wanted to believe things with my mom would be different. We never discussed what happened to his dad's marriage to the assistant he had left his mom for. I figured like any marriage that started in disaster, it ended the same way. I hated thinking about how my mom may go through the same thing they had.

Regardless of what poor decisions Jasper had made in the past, it wasn't my place to warn her of his past, no matter how bright and blinding the red flags were waving in my mind. I didn't want to be the wedge that was driven between the two of them. If it wasn't going to work out between them, I wanted it to be because they had given it everything they had, and they learned they weren't meant for each other.

I still couldn't help thinking about how she would react, though, if and when she found out about my relationship with Brix.

CHAPTER TWENTY

BRIX

After the night I drove Ivy down to the beach, all I could think about was bringing her to our house in Myrtle Beach for a weekend. When my dad mentioned going out of town for work and that Charlene was joining, I decided it was the perfect opportunity for us to get away.

Fourth of July had come and gone. Soon Ivy would be heading back to school, so I knew I only had a few more weeks left before she'd be gone. In the back of my mind, between everything going on with my mom and the band, I managed to push my argument with Tysin earlier this summer to the recesses of my mind. The one where I bet him I could sleep with her, sending her back to school with a broken heart.

When I'm with Ivy, the way I feel just being near her and the feelings that have begun to grow more intensely, it's so easy to close out everything else and focus on being in the moment with her. I didn't want to think about the hurtful comments I had said before I'd had a chance to truly get to know her.

On the drive to Myrtle Beach, with her hand wrapped in mine, I decide I need to use our time alone together to sit down and tell her the truth. Having Ivy around has changed me for the better in so many ways. I was selfish and inconsiderate. I only cared about myself and the band. I didn't give a shit about the women I slept with, their feelings, or anyone I hurt. If it got me what I wanted in the end, that's all that mattered to me.

Now, here I am thinking through all the ways I'll explain to her how selfish I had been and how I had planned to hurt her. I want to open up to her about how I feel, but how do I begin to tell her when there is a large part of this that could hurt her, too?

I want my words to mean something, not be covered up by the cloud of betrayal hanging over me. I know she'll be angry and hurt, but I hope she'll give me a chance to prove to her the things I said and the way I felt in the beginning, isn't at all how I feel about her now.

"Oh my God, this house is beautiful." Ivy's eyes light up, staring out the window as we pull up the long driveway.

The little things that make her happy and smile have become the best part of my day. I'll start to do whatever I can just to see this look on her face.

Putting the truck in park, I tell her to stay where she is as I jog around to her side and open the door, holding my hand out to her.

"You can be so romantic." She tries to cover up her grin as I pull her into me, kissing her softly. Her hand wraps around the base of my neck, holding me to her.

Grabbing our bags, I slam the door shut and slide my fingers into hers with a wink. "Whatever you say, baby."

She rests her head on my shoulder while I sort through my keys, trying to find the right one. Slipping the key in the lock, I push the door open, letting Ivy lead the way.

"Oh my..." Her voice trails off as she walks through the house, running her hand along the back of the white couch over to the counter wrapped around the large eat-in kitchen.

"Are you sure we can't live here?"

Despite her soft laugh and her wide smile, there's an edge of seriousness in her tone. If we could stay here, I'd have our shit moved over in a heartbeat.

As I set our bags down in the foyer, Ivy unlocks the sliding glass door and pushes it open, stepping out onto the patio overlooking the ocean.

The sun shines above us, not a single cloud floats in the sky. Her burnt-orange dress leaves most of her back on display. She does a twirl, arms held out around her with her head thrown back.

"You like it here?"

"Like it? I think it's safe to say I love it. Thank you for bringing me here."

It ended up working out perfectly as it was the one weekend over the next few weeks that we had no shows. It took some convincing, but Jayde was able to give her some time off. I told her there was no choice, she was going to be here either way. She owed me a favor after the size of the crowds we had been bringing in the place.

We decide to head down to the beach. I'm not one to go swimming in the ocean, at least not since I was younger. However, I know how Ivy looks in a swimsuit, and there's not much I wouldn't do to see her in one again.

Her eyes keep traveling back to me, specifically my shirtless chest, as I spread out our blanket in the sand. She unwraps the sarong around her waist, showing off her sexy-as-hell legs as she moves to sit down.

Setting the umbrella up, she pulls out her sunscreen and begins rubbing it over her chest and stomach. I'm distracted watching her hands move. She doesn't catch on right away until she looks up, noticing I'm blocking the sunlight.

"You want to help me?"

"Fuck yes," I mutter, as an older woman who is sitting nearby with her young children whips her head in my direction. She gives me a glare that says, "Say that again, and I'll drown you in the ocean."

Ivy's eyes widen as she tries to conceal her laugh.

"I mean, heck yes." I laugh, falling to my knees as I crawl behind her. She squirts some of the sunscreen in my palm, and I begin to rub it over her back and shoulders. She moves her hair out of the way, tilting her head to the side as I lean forward, pressing a soft kiss against her skin.

"Do you know how hard it is for me to keep my hands in all the appropriate places right now?"

"Hmm," she says, her eyes meeting mine. "How hard?"

She drags her lower lip between her teeth, and my dick grows at the visual.

"Very fucking hard," I growl low enough for only her to hear me.

"You're lookin' pretty damn good yourself." Her hands wrap around my legs on either side of her.

We spend a few hours down by the water. When I notice the apples of her cheeks turning rosy, we decide to call it a day.

I'm flipping the burgers on the grill when Ivy strolls out wearing the same dress she had on earlier that day, folding her legs beneath her when she takes a seat on the lounge chair.

"Where do you see this going between us?"

The uncertainty in her voice with her question takes me by surprise.

"What do you mean?" Holding the spatula out, I flip the last burger before closing the grill again, setting it down on the counter.

"Like, what is this to you? I leave for school in a little over three weeks. I guess I'm wondering where you see this going when the summer is over?"

"Well..." I sigh, walking over to where she's sitting. Holding my hand out to her, I help her up, taking a seat waiting for her to crawl into my lap.

As soon as she's situated, I wrap my arm around her using my other hand to trace a line along her back.

Her hair is pulled back, leaving little strands of hair falling to frame her face. Holding the glass of wine in her hand, she runs her lip along the edge as she takes another swallow, finishing the rest of the contents.

"I know I don't want this to end," I answer honestly.

Her eyes soften at the words, a sense of ease coming from her.

"It won't be easy waking up and not having you here with me. That's the part I think about the most."

"Me, too."

"But I can come to you during the week or between shows, and you can come visit when you get the chance."

She nods.

"We'll make it work, Ivy. Whatever we have to do, okay? We'll make it work."

"Okay."

She still seems hesitant and seeing it makes me nervous. Nervous for what I'm planning to tell her this weekend, nervous about how she'll react, and worried if she'll believe that I don't feel the same way now.

Her eyes search for something aimlessly on the ground, growing distant. I wait for her to collect her thoughts or for her to tell me what's on her mind, but it never comes. She rests her body against me. Unable to resist, I press kisses against her shoulder, feeling the heat radiate from her skin from the sun she got earlier that day.

"What are you thinking about?"

"Huh?" she asks, her eyes snapping back to me, pulling her from her thoughts. "Oh, I was just thinking about what you said."

"What part?"

"Just coming to see each other. What it will be like, I guess."

I feel like there's more she's not saying.

"Talk to me," I murmur, moving to look her in the eyes.

"I guess I'm curious how things were when I first got to town. The people you were hanging out with, the things you were doing. You're not going to go back to that, are you?"

She doesn't spell it out exactly, but I know she's talking about me bringing home the girl from the bar and sleeping with her. She wants reassurance I'm not going to go back to living the single life, and I can't say I blame her for wondering.

"Are you asking if I'm going to go back to fucking around?"

She doesn't respond, but the look on her face says everything words don't.

"Fuck no, Ivy. Are you kidding me?"

"What do you expect me to think, Brix?" She pushes off me to stand, holding her arms out beside her. "Up until recently, I was just some big joke to you. Things have been so good between us, but I constantly feel like I'm waiting for the moment when it all changes, when I find out you've been fucking with me this whole time."

The hurt and fear on her face are like an iron fist to the gut. Especially knowing she's not wrong in her fears.

My own worries about how I'm going to find a way of telling her the truth creep in, and I know right now is not the time or place. I need more time to show her how I feel, to prove to her she can trust me.

I'm terrified if I were to tell her now, she'd never believe me. Why would she? Everything I've ever said and done has proven otherwise.

I hope, whatever I do, that in the end, it's enough to convince her how sorry I am because I'm scared, if it's not, I'll lose her forever.

CHAPTER TWENTY-ONE

IVY

After our conversation last night, I think Brix picked up on my hesitance about where things are going between us. One minute he was the man I had spent nearly half of my life loathing, then when we're forced together for the summer, it's like all my thoughts became a jumbled mess.

There were times when I thought I wouldn't make it to the end of the summer without killing him, then there were others where I felt a pull so strong and a connection so real, I started to doubt myself and what I had thought about him for all those years.

I hated to admit it, but it made me insecure and question everything. On one hand, I wanted to push all the worries aside and enjoy whatever this is, but on the other hand, there were real fears in my mind that this was still some sort of joke to him.

Waking up next to Brix is something I will never get sick of doing. I felt him stir this morning as he slipped out of bed, still naked from the night before.

"You can go back to sleep. I'm going to go downstairs and call my mom."

Nodding my head, I pull the blanket up under my chin, rolling over on my stomach. He leans forward to press a kiss against my forehead, his mouth lingering before he pulls back, staring down at me.

He smiles softly, sleep still present in his beautiful brown eyes. My eyes rake over his body before rolling onto my back, tossing my arm out toward him.

"You're making it hard for me not to crawl back into bed next to you."

"I wouldn't complain one bit."

He grins. "Give me a few, and I'll be right back."

I nod, smiling back at him as he presses his knee down on the bed leaning over to kiss me. It's quick, before he pulls back, turning to pull on a pair of shorts as he sneaks out the door.

It doesn't take me long to doze off back to sleep. The breeze flowing in from the beach, the waves crashing against the shore in the distance, brings a quiet peacefulness. A little while later, I wake with the scent of sausage and bacon lingering in the air as Brix whispers my name, urging me to wake up.

Peeking one eye open, he's fully dressed now looking like he had jumped out of the shower not too long ago. His hair is still damp as he carries a tray with a plate of food and a pitcher of orange juice.

"Good morning." He grins, pausing to stare at me from where the sheets now sit partially covering my lower half. His eyes linger on my body, biting on his lip ring, sucking it into his mouth before his eyes find their way back to mine.

"I hope you're hungry," he hums, setting the tray on top of my legs.

Sitting up, I stretch my arms over my head, letting my hair cascade down my back. Swiping a piece of bacon, I take a bite as I moan. It's been so long since I've eaten bacon. My student budget settles for what's easy and affordable, resorting to cereal and milk or pop tarts for the mornings when I was up entirely too late.

"This looks amazing."

Brix sits on the bed near my feet, digging in to his plate sitting next to mine. We sit in silence as we both eat.

"How is your mom doing?"

He takes a few seconds, looking lost in his thoughts while he considers how to respond. "She seemed good. Lighter, happier. She's ready to be home, though. I can tell she's getting antsy."

"Have you thought about going to see her?"

"They actually want me to start doing counseling sessions before she goes home. I'm waiting to find out when exactly."

"That's good. I'm sure she's looking forward to seeing you."

"I am, too. I don't even remember the last time I saw my mom sober. It's been years, honestly."

My heart clenches in my chest at the sound of his words, the ache and sadness at the admission. My dad took off when I was young because he simply didn't want the responsibility of having a child. My mom mentioned he struggled with addiction when they were married. I've thought about what it would be like if he hadn't taken off, how our relationship would've been, and how having him in my life would've shaped me.

There's a very real possibility if he had stayed, Brix and I would be going through very similar paths with our parents.

"I'm here for you. You know, if you need or want to talk, or if you don't."

He takes a bite of his toast, chewing quietly as he nods his head. "I know. I appreciate it, too."

After breakfast, Brix takes the tray downstairs and takes care of cleaning up the dishes while I escape to the bathroom to shower. We decide since today is our last day in Myrtle Beach, we'll get out of the house and do some sightseeing.

I've visited here before, but I was much younger and don't really remember it. We walk from our house to downtown, taking in some of the shops and bars along the boardwalk.

Being away from home, away from the people, it's almost like we're two different people. Brix, the once wild bad boy with a reputation for spending his nights with random women, is seemingly the attentive boyfriend.

He held my hand, kissed me without thought, and made me laugh more times than I can count. We joked about my taste in music when I told him I still enjoy listening to some of the country music I grew up on.

When I see the spark hit his eye and his smile stretch across his face, for a moment, I'm lost in thought, thinking about how perfect this weekend has been and how I wouldn't trade it for the world.

I try to push out of my mind how it's all going to change when we leave here and head back home. While we'll still have our moments together, we still have the secret of who we are and what we're going to contend with.

After we grab dinner, we decide to take another walk along the boardwalk, overlooking the ocean.

"Want to go for a ride?" Brix asks, his eyebrow quips deviously.

For a second, my mind goes to a dirtier version of what he could mean until a sly grin stretches across his face, pointing to the Ferris wheel.

"I mean, go on that ride." He chuckles. "Although, if you have other ideas in mind, who am I to deny you what you want?"

Pressing my lips together, I shake my head as I playfully push on his chest. Reaching for my hand, he reels me back until I fall against his chest. His arms band around me, holding me close as he leans in to whisper, "Think of all the naughty things I could do to you up there."

I gasp at the thought, staring up at the Ferris wheel moving above us. Each car is covered with blue glass surrounding it. While you could very much see through it, there's still plenty that can't be seen at a hundred eighty feet in the air.

"Like what?"

He doesn't bother to look around him, careful of who may hear him as he replies, "For starters, I want those sexy as fuck legs spread open for me while I feel you cum around my fingers."

Instantly, my face heats at the visual he's put in my mind. I picture Brix kneeling in front of me, as the Ferris wheel moves, with my legs spread open for only him to see.

His eyes blaze, recognizing where my thoughts have drifted, too, as his hand wraps in mine, tugging me with him toward where the line starts. Each long second that ticks by as we wait feels excruciating.

I rub my thighs together, rocking my ass against his Brix, feeling his hard cock against the curve of my ass. He tilts his head forward, blowing his hot breath against the column of my neck.

"Do you know how fucking hard you're making me right now?"

"No..." I trail off, tilting my head toward his.

"Hard enough that if you keep that shit up, I'm going to cum in my fuckin' pants in front of all these damn people," he grunts harshly, stealing my breath with every word.

Brix does dirty talk very well. No matter who is around to see or hear, the thoughts and images he puts in my mind can turn me up to another level.

When we are finally next in line, Brix doesn't wait for the man to hold the door open for us, helping me into the lift and pulling me into his lap.

The sexual tension must be thick around us, as the operator laughs before slamming the door shut behind us.

With each rider joining, we move higher and higher into the sky. Wrapping my arm around Brix, my fingers rake through the hair at the base of his neck, kissing my way up toward his ear.

"Now that you have me here, what are you going to do with me?"

Brix trails his fingers over my knee, up my thigh to the edge of my shorts. Once his fingers reach the apex of my thigh, he drives me wild when he runs his finger back down my leg forcing my body to tremble with need.

My breath comes out heavily with each stroke of his fingertips. When he reaches the hem of my shorts once again, my legs fall open further, tempting him.

"Please," I plead quietly, begging him to touch me where I want to feel him most. I grind down on him, earning me a heavy growl.

"Ivy," he grunts.

"Brix, please," I cry. We're slowly reaching the top, and all I can think about is him touching me. I don't give a shit where we are or who can see us, I want him to put me out of my misery right here.

He continues his slow and agonizing torture of dragging his fingers over my legs, loving how my body reacts to him. His mouth kisses his way up my neck, as my fingers grip his hair, holding him to me.

When his fingers reach my upper thigh once again, I reach down, clenching my hand around his.

"If you don't touch me, I will."

Groaning, he mutters, "Fuck," before he finally gives in to me. When I let go of his hand, he stops, telling me he wants me to help him.

I'm in a daze, not following what he means at first before folding my hand over his. Adjusting my legs over his thighs, keeping them spread open, he guides our hands along the edge of my panties, tracing them.

My stomach clenches with anticipation when his finger grazes along my wet core, as he murmurs in my ear about how badly he wants me right now. The sound of blood rushing through my body sends me into a spiral. The thought of what we're doing, the possibility of someone seeing or being caught sends a spike of adrenaline gushing through me.

His hand slips under my panties, brushing over my clit. I tilt my head back against his shoulder, feeling my body tremor with need.

"So wet," he mutters. "So fucking sexy."

Moving my hand over his, I guide him down closer to where I want him to be. When his large finger slips inside of me, my entire body shudders, squeezing my eyes shut.

I hear the distant sound of people around us laughing and the faint hum of music playing below, but it all falls away in this moment with Brix. The basket we're riding in jolts as it moves a few feet. My heart hammers in my chest, chancing a peek at the world around us and the boardwalk below, wondering if anyone can see us.

"Do you really think I'd let anyone see you like this?"

He doesn't wait for me to respond, his eyes blazing into me when I peer up at him.

"Not a fucking chance." His words are low, so full of desire. My pussy clenches around his finger as he adds his thumb rubbing over my clit.

"You're driving me crazy."

Each subtle flick of his finger tracing over my sensitive skin causes my stomach to quiver. He alternates between rubbing my clit to slowly torturing me with his finger, each move unpredictable but delivered with precision.

He knows how to work me up to the point I'm damn near begging.

“Brix,” I pant.

The basket moves again, sending us closer and closer to the bottom. My body is wound tight with need. I’m so close to the edge.

Brix adjusts his hand, curling his finger inside me as he brushes his thumb over my tight bud once again. The move, combined with the soft feel of his teeth grazing against my shoulder, barely containing his moan as he rocks his hips against my ass, sends me spiraling over the cliff.

Squeezing my eyes shut tight, I struggle to breathe, the air changing as the sun beats down on us.

“So mine,” he growls, crashing his mouth on mine in a soul-searing kiss.

All I can do is wrap my hand around his neck as I hold on for the ride.

CHAPTER TWENTY-TWO

BRIX

Jogging down the front steps, I run my hand over the front of my pants, checking to make sure I have my phone. I'm reaching for the handle of my pickup, swinging the door open when I hear the soft purr of an engine pull up behind me, spotting my dad's Lexus pull into the driveway.

"Hey, Son."

I want to roll my eyes at his jovial response. We've hardly spoken to each other since he dropped his surprise marriage on me, now he wants to show up here like everything is perfect?

I guess when you're Jasper Ward and you live in a world with rose-colored glasses, focusing only on yourself, you tend to forget it's not sunshine and rainbows for everyone else around you.

"Hi," I reply. No sunshine. No rainbows. Just his son, standing here wishing he'd move his fucking car so I can leave.

"You headin' off somewhere?" he asks. His olive skin is darker, likely from all the vacationing he's been doing over the past few weeks. I want to curl my lip in annoyance, but when I think about how I've spent the past few weeks since he's been gone, I can't find it in me to be bothered.

With him away, it's given me and Ivy space to enjoy ourselves without the watchful eyes of our parents around.

"Meeting up with the guys. Band practice."

He nods, surveying the yard and the landscaping I had installed last week, making his way to the front of the house.

I know the terms of our deal. I haven't let shit go around here, yet I'm waiting for him to say something condescending that'll have me biting my tongue to avoid telling him off.

Let him say what he's here to say, then send him on his way.

"I won't keep you. I just wanted to stop by and talk to you about your mom."

I break eye contact with him, pinching my lips together, stopping myself from shaking my head.

Anytime he brings her up, it turns into an argument. He wanted out of their marriage, the way I see it, how she's doing or where she's at is none of his concern.

"I saw your Uncle Travis down at Miller's the other day when I dropped my car off to have it serviced. He told me." He pauses. "Why didn't you tell me what was going on, Brix?"

"There's nothing for me to say. Not to you, anyway."

He winces, looking wounded as he glances down at the ground, nodding his head even though I know it's more in acceptance than agreeance. I've upset him, and for a second, I consider asking him why it bothers him?

"Maybe that's true. I lost the right to ask about her years ago, but I still care about your mother. You may not believe me, but I do."

I force a chuckle, turning away from him to look for Ivy. She was supposed to be coming with me, but now she's nowhere in sight.

"I'm proud of you, Brix." I rear back, regarding him with furrowed brows. He must see the disbelief on my face, a look of guilt passing over his. "I may not have told you in a while, but it doesn't mean it's not true."

"You have an interesting way of showing it."

"I take a lot of blame for where things are now. Between me. With your mother. That's on me. You've carried a lot of the weight of our divorce, and I'm sorry. I'm proud of the man you are, the man you've become. I couldn't convince her to seek help, but she is now. She has you, and it's because of you, she's going to pull through this."

I blink back the tears threatening to fill the brim of my eyes. He's struck a chord.

"You've been there for her. You've welcomed Ivy. She told me how you helped her with her car. Thank you," he says, his voice trailing off at the end.

I nod, rubbing the bridge of my nose. He takes a step toward me, pulling me into a hug.

The sound of the door closing behind us has us both taking a step back, turning toward the house. Ivy is standing there, eyes wide and staring between the two of us.

"Ivy, hello. It's good to see you."

"You, too, Jasper!" She looks to me, concern etching her face, searching mine for the answers she's looking for. I mouth, "it's okay," to her, which helps in the moment.

"What are you up to?"

"Oh, I'm just going with Brix to check out his band practice." Ivy hesitates, not sure if that's the right answer, but it's the safe one.

Remembering what he said just a moment ago about welcoming Ivy, I wonder if he's trying to piece together all the many ways I've been there for Ivy since she moved to Carolina Beach.

If she has an itch, I've been there to help scratch it. Maybe not literally, but figuratively.

"Well, I will get out of here. You two have a good night."

He walks backward to the car, opening the door as he climbs in. Motioning to Ivy to get in, she nods nervously, jogging to the door.

"What happened?" she asks incredulously. "You had me freaked out for a second. You looked upset."

Her hair is curled, part of it pulled up with the rest down hanging over her shoulder in waves.

She must be wearing some sort of lipstick that makes her lips look shiny, which distracts me momentarily as I'm lost in thought of kissing her, wanting to taste her.

"Brix…" She waits. "Is everything okay?"

"Everything's fine, I promise. Just shit with my mom. Let's get out of here."

"Okay." She pauses, sounding more like a question. She ducks to check the rearview mirror. Seeing my father has pulled out and driven off, she slides across the bench seat closer to me, before buckling herself in.

It's not until I back out and put the car in drive when I reach my hand down, resting it against her thigh, that the tension finally eases up.

She doesn't press me as we make the trip across town over to Tysin's house, which I'm thankful for. She knows when to push me and when to give me space. Right now, I just need time to digest our conversation.

"I think that's Kyla's car." Ivy points to the car parked in Tysin's drive.

Glancing at the cars parked along the street, I search for any sign of Madden or why Kyla may be here when he's not around.

"This could get interesting," I joke, turning the truck off and climbing out, holding my hand out to Ivy as she slides out behind me.

"What the heck is she doing here?"

She's caught off guard when I grab her hand, slipping my fingers through hers, pulling her with me.

"Probably the same thing we do when we're alone." Flashing her a wink, she presses her lips together to smother her grin.

I don't bother waiting for Tysin to answer the door, knowing damn well he's expecting me. Pounding my fist on the solid oak, I reach for the handle, stepping back to let Ivy lead the way.

"Ivy?" Kyla asks incredulously, pushing away from Tysin who's leaning against the kitchen counter. His hands are braced against the marble countertop, not bothering to disguise the fact something was clearly going on between them.

It's as if he's dangling the fact he's been messing around with Kyla right in front of Madden, waiting for the moment he catches them. She's an adult and capable of making decisions for herself, but we both know with Tysin's history with women, Madden won't be happy about it.

For a second, I contemplate calling him out on it, and judging by the way his eyes bounce between Ivy and me, he knows the easier rebuttal. Clenching my jaw, narrowing my eyes on him, warning him not to say a word.

I still haven't figured out how to talk to her about the bet. I hate even calling it that.

Every time I think about it, the fear of her walking away the way my dad did my mom creeps in. She has every right to know the truth, every right to walk away, but like the bastard I am, I want to hold onto her for a little while longer.

I can't hear what Ivy and Kyla are talking about, but judging by their whispered words, it has to do with the two of us. Kyla's eyes bounce from Tysin, over to me, then back to Ivy as she shuffles from side to side.

None of us know what to say, how to explain or justify our relationships, so instead, I change the subject entirely.

"You talk to Madden yet? I don't want to sit around here all fucking day. Let's get this show on the road."

Tysin leads the way through the kitchen, down the hall heading to his basement where our equipment is set up. For a second, I expect Kyla to take off, not wanting to be here when her brother shows up, but she doesn't.

As soon as Tysin bought his house, we immediately went to work on soundproofing it, giving us a space to practice.

He still wants to make a booth where we can record our music, but we need to save up more before we do.

Our priority is to cut our demo. Something we can send out to the major record labels. The only other hope we have of getting seen is if we get lucky and someone finds us on social media. Kyla's been helping us out, capturing videos at our shows, and uploading them on social media.

I hear Kyla whisper to Ivy, asking her what's going on between us. Bending down, I plug the microphone into the speaker as Tysin picks up his guitar doing the same.

My eyes find Ivy's across the room as she and Kyla take a seat on the couch directly across from where our makeshift stage is set up. I focus my ear to her, waiting to hear her answer.

"Things are good," she says, not breaking eye contact. "We're friendly..." Her voice trails off.

The steps creak, and I see Kyla's eyes widen, darting over to Tysin before looking up at where her brother jogs down the stairs.

"Yo," he says, tossing his keys onto the table, pausing to look over at Kyla sitting on the couch. "What are you doing here?"

He stops, looking at her and around to the two of us. I hold my hands up, signaling for him to not bother asking me. I'm staying out of this. Turning back toward the speaker, I busy myself with plugging in the rest of our equipment.

Having Ivy here, it's like my body is on hyperalert. Every time she moves, I sense her near me. Whenever I glance her way, I always find her looking back at me.

"I met Ivy here. She mentioned how Brix had helped her with her car. I wanted to have him look at mine." Kyla's eyes dart to mine as I stand, looking over at Madden. He's in the middle of adjusting the height on his drum throne.

"Ahh, yeah," I mutter, not sure what to say. "She mentioned she thought her oil was leaking. I told her I'd take a look before she took it into the shop."

Madden's holding his drumsticks in front of him, pausing before he takes a seat.

"Why didn't you just ask me? I could've come over to look at it for you."

"I just didn't want to bother you." Kyla's tongue darts out, wetting her lips as she rubs them together. She knows she's caught in a lie, but she keeps on adding to it until she ends up spiraling out of control.

"So, you thought it wouldn't bother Brix, but asking your brother was too much?"

"Brix owed me one," she spits out like her mouth is on fire if she doesn't get it out.

"Oh," he says, brows bunched together as he looks between us. Tysin has the nerve to chuckle under his breath, adjusting the strap of his guitar on his shoulder. He sticks his pick in his mouth like he has all the time in the world to wait on this conversation.

Meanwhile, not one person has brought up his name, suspecting he's the person she was here to see. How did I get roped into this shit?

"I put in a good word for him with my best friend. He owes me," Kyla jokes, plastering a fake smile on her face, clapping her hand on Ivy's knee.

Madden drops it, taking a seat and hits the pedal on his drums, checking the sound. I tug on my microphone cord, giving it more length to move around. Ivy's eyes blaze into me, her leg bouncing on the floor.

She reaches her hand up, tucking a long strand of her brown hair behind her ear. She's dressed in a sexy cobalt-blue tank top and black denim shorts. Her toenails are painted a bright pink, which is a color I've never seen her wear before, but it's sexy on her.

Kyla's too busy trying to hide the fact she can't take her eyes off Tysin as I mouth to Ivy, "friendly?" She bites her lip to cover up her laugh when I quirk my brow at her, earning me a shrug.

"I'll make you my best friend later," I mouth slowly, hoping she can make out what I'm saying.

This time she doesn't try to hold back the grin from stretching across her face and fuck me if I don't love seeing how happy the thought of us together makes her.

"Can't wait," she mouths back.

For the rest of our band practice, she sits, never taking her eyes off me, with her leg bouncing to the beat of the music and a smile on her face that makes me feel like there is nowhere else in the world she'd rather be.

CHAPTER TWENTY-THREE

IVY

"I'll take a panty ripper." Brix winks, leaning over the bar reaching for my hand.

Since we got back from Myrtle Beach, we've been playing with fire. Where we were once careful about showing PDA and who could be around to see us, has since gone out the window.

Brix has never been one to give a shit what people say or think. Just like now, as his fingers wrap around mine, pressing a kiss against my skin. Goose bumps spread up my arms from his touch alone.

Even standing here, in a crowded bar, the look on his face and the way his lips feel on my skin, it's like it's only the two of us.

"Panty ripper, huh?" I quirk my brow, gazing at his mouth for a moment before staring him in the eyes. Reaching for the bottle of coconut rum, preparing to mix his drink, I question, "Isn't that a little fruity for you?"

"I wasn't talking about the drink, baby."

When he winks at me, a shiver shoots down my body. Putting the bottle back, I reach into the cooler to grab a chilled glass and fill it with beer before sliding it across the counter to him.

"Is that a no?"

"That's a wait until tonight."

He bites down on his lip, dragging his lip ring into his mouth, and I imagine doing the very same thing.

"When is your break?"

"Break? I got here twenty minutes ago."

"I think you've been working very hard." He accentuates the word hard with a firm voice, eyes widening as he wags his brows suggestively.

"Hard, huh?"

"Mmmhm, very hard. You deserve a few minutes to relax." He looks past me to Jayde and yells, "Jayde, it's time my girl gets a break. She's overworked right now, and it's bullshit."

"Shut up, Ward. Don't you have music to play or some shit?"

She doesn't look up from the drink she's mixing to address him. I just laugh.

"I guess she's right," he jokes. "I'll make it up to you later, though."

Brix grabs his beer, taking a step back from the bar and turns to head over to the table with the guys. They don't go on for about thirty minutes, but the atmosphere is starting to fill with anticipation.

They play here often, no matter how much they do, they still manage to pull in a crowd of people from all over North Carolina to see them live.

I notice we're running low on ice, so I head into the back to get more. Before I do, I make a quick run to the bathroom near where Brix and his bandmates and friends are sitting.

After getting through the line and quickly washing my hands, I opt to take the hall passing by them, wanting to wish him good luck before his set.

"I hate to break it to you, but it looks like it's she who has you eating out of the palm of her hand!" Tysin shouts over the music, cackling.

"Shut the fuck up," Brix mutters.

"Well, looks like you've won part of the bet. You fucked her."

Overhearing the word bet pauses me in my tracks. My heart feels like it fell into a pit at the bottom of my stomach, the knot wrapping around it twisting further.

What bet? What the hell is he talking about?

"I'm waiting for the part where you send her ass heart-broken back to wherever the hell she came from, though."

"I said shut the fuck up, you stupid motherfucker. You hear me?" Brix seethes. The anger is at a level I've never heard from him before. What I don't hear is how he's arguing he's wrong, denying every word that comes out of his mouth.

Taking a step back, I turn to go the other way through the back of the bar. Tears fill my eyes, but I do my best to fight them off with everything in me.

How could I have been so stupid?

It was only last weekend I had told Brix how scared I was, waiting for the moment when I found out this had been nothing but a joke to him. Now everything I feared has become a reality.

All night I tried to put the thoughts out of my mind. Thankfully, Brix and the guys went on stage shortly after, and I didn't have to face him right away. I didn't think I'd be able to fake my way through it until we had a chance to talk later.

I knew if he found out I overheard, his anger would only be worse. I didn't want to do this with him before they were supposed to play. Whatever this was about would have to wait until later.

I kept coming back to what Tysin said. How he had made a bet to not only fuck me but to break my heart at the same time. I was nothing but a joke to him.

A joke.

The word twisted like a knife every time I thought about it.

"Are you okay?" Oaklyn asks later that night. "Ever since you came back from getting ice, you've acted like something is bothering you. Did something happen? You good?"

Taking a heavy breath, I nod. Not even sure how to say it. I don't even think I could without breaking down.

"I'm just not feeling very well is all."

"Are you sure? Do you want to sit down? You look as white as a sheet."

She leads me over to the barstool in the back room, pushing a glass of ice water in my hand, forcing me to drink.

"Just sit for a minute, will ya? We'll be fine for a bit if you need a break or something."

"Yeah. Okay." I nod, holding the glass up to my lips. Sweat dots my forehead, my hands clammy. Leaning my head against the wall, I stare through the doorway toward the stage where Brix and the guys play. I think back to the first night, the way he flirted with the women in the front of the crowd, gyrating against their hands, letting them feel him up as he sang.

He hasn't been doing it anymore. In fact, he hasn't since before the night he brought home the blonde-haired girl. My mind sifts through all the memories, the nights we spent together, looking for any sign or clues that would've signaled this was going on.

I think what hurts most of all is there are none. Once we finally gave in to each other, to the temptation that had been dangling in front of us, it was like the Brix I once knew was gone.

He still had his asshole moments and tendencies, but behind all of it, he made me believe he cared. Even when I broke down the night at the beach house and exposed all my concerns and worries, he pulled me back into his lap and assured me there was nothing to fear.

He lied to me, and just like he had set out to do, he had broken me.

Finishing what's left of my drink, I toss the cup in the trash and do my best to pull myself from the darkness for the rest of the night.

"Hey, girl." Kyla smiles as she slides up against the bar. Her phone is in her hand, her fingers typing furiously across the screen.

"Hey," I mutter, with barely enough energy to shout over the music. She picks up on my mood, her eyes narrowing as she tilts her head to look at me as if asking me what's wrong.

I roll my eyes, plastering a fake smile on my face, as I lean in to ask her what she wants to drink. She orders a martini. Her eyes bore into me as I go through the motions of preparing it for her.

She doesn't say anything as I help the crowd of people at the bar.

"What's wrong with you?"

"Nothing. Everything. I don't even know."

"That sounds like a whole lot of I need a fucking drink."

I nod. "There's so much to tell you. I can't possibly go into it all right now."

Jayde looks down the bar at me, glaring. We're busy, and I know it's her way of saying focus more on helping customers and less on talking to my friend. I promise Kyla I'll catch her up when my shift is over.

Although, the more I think about it, the more I want to go straight home and not think about anything at all.

It's after midnight when my shift ends. The crowd died down a little bit as the night went on. I contemplate staying after to talk to Brix, to confront him and Tysin about everything, but I don't have the energy right now.

After punching out, I thank Oaklyn for helping pick up my slack tonight and split my tip money with her. She knew something was off with me and didn't bat an eye at helping carry more of the load. When she refuses to take the money, I shove it in her pocket before turning and walking out, not giving her any choice.

A Rebels Havoc is playing in my car; their playlist still up from my drive to work earlier. I want to turn it off, I even reach my hand out for the button when I pull back.

The tears I've fought back all night fill my eyes once more, only this time I let them flow free. I give myself time to feel the emotions before I lock it up and focus on how I am going to move on.

I know what I have to do from here. It isn't going to be easy. In fact, it is probably going to break me, but I'll never let him know.

I'll never let him see me broken. He doesn't deserve to know he got through to me.

CHAPTER TWENTY-FOUR

BRIX

I didn't believe Jayde when she told me Ivy took off after her shift. I thought surely she'd let me know before she'd leave. I tried calling her several times on my drive home, each call going straight to voice mail.

A wave of relief washes over me pulling in the driveway. Although every light in the house is off, her car is parked where it normally sits.

Oaklyn mentioned she thought maybe she wasn't feeling well, but it didn't explain why she didn't bother to text me. Pushing all thoughts aside, I walk into the house and jog up the stairs heading straight for her room.

When I open her door, I expect to find her in the middle of her bed, curled up in a ball with a blanket pulled over her, like usual. An unshakeable sense settles over me that something is wrong when I find her bed perfectly made, left untouched.

Shutting the door behind me, I race down the hall, opening the door to my bedroom. The lights are turned down low. It is still dark, but there's enough light for me to see her and make out what she's wearing.

She moves her leg, crossing one over top of the other. My eyes zero in on the heels on her feet, remembering them from the first night she was in town. She points her toe, causing the muscles in her legs to flex, and all I can think about is kissing every inch from her ankle to her thigh.

Stepping in closer, my eyes fall to her chest and the black nightie she's wearing.

"Everything okay?" My voice comes out hoarse. The fear I felt a moment ago is now replaced with desire, seeing what she's wearing, knowing she was waiting for me to come home.

She doesn't answer, but I see her subtle nod.

Holding my hand out to her, I help her stand, watching her turn to show me the backside of her outfit. I groan seeing the crisscross of the ties along her back down to the barely-there scrap of material covering her pussy.

"Sit." Her words are firm, commanding, pointing to the chair sitting in the middle of my room. I had been so focused on her, I hadn't even noticed it until she pointed it out.

Pulling my shirt over my head, I toss it behind me, not bothering to pay attention to where it lands.

She steps behind me, holding out a scarf in her hand. It takes me a second, but when the smell of coconut hits my nose, I realize it's the wrap she wore at the beach. Using it to cover my eyes, I'm bathed in darkness. Grabbing each of my hands, she moves them, forcing them to grip the edge of the seat.

"Don't move your hands, or I stop. Understand?"

I want to press timeout, ask her if she's okay, if we're okay, but the moment her mouth trails along the column of my neck, all rational thoughts are out the window.

Her hands are on my waist, unbuttoning my pants, guiding them down around my ankles.

It's quiet for a moment, hearing a subtle click in the distance before music begins playing, soft at first until the volume is turned up louder. My body settles into the chair, my fingers clenching the hardwood in anticipation.

I feel something warm and wet dripping on my thighs before her hands glide over me, massaging the warm oil into my skin, starting near my knee, traveling up my leg. She continues to rub her fingers, tracing a line hovering dangerously close to my aching cock before sliding back down again. Each time she gets closer and closer to touching me. Just when I think she may put me out of my misery, her hand begins to travel away from where I want her.

"Fuck, baby," I moan, "I want to feel your mouth on me so damn bad."

She doesn't respond, doesn't make a move to wrap her hand around my dick. She just continues to massage the warm liquid into my thighs, over my abs, and into my chest.

She trails her fingers back down my stomach, brushing over the tip of my cock. I bite down on my lower lip, the subtle touch of her hand on me turns me on more. My leg begins to bounce, my stomach clenching with need.

As if reading my mind, her hand wraps around the base of my cock, tight, as she pumps.

"Ahhhh, fuck," I mutter, thrusting my hips up into her touch. Her hands are warm, sliding over me with ease as she pumps. "Fuck, fuck. Baby, your hand feels so fucking good," I groan.

Her hand alternates between moving slow over the tip, before tightening and jerking me harder. I'm on the brink, feeling like my orgasm is within reach, when her hand lets go, leaving me forcing a heavy breath.

I wish I could see her, touch her. I want to feel her skin and kiss her lips.

"I want to feel you so damn bad," I moan again.

"Where?"

"Everywhere."

"You're going to have to be more specific if you want me to continue."

"I want to feel your pussy wrapped around me, squeezing me like a fucking vise. I want your mouth on mine and your arms around my neck. I want to feel you milking me until we both cum. Is that fucking good enough? Get on top of me. Right. Now."

She doesn't say anything, as I feel her skin brush against my leg, her warm hands grab onto my shoulders. I don't know what I thought she was doing, but when I feel her pussy lower onto me, my eyes damn near roll into the back of my head.

"Kiss me," I moan, wanting to feel her lips on mine.

Her hands grip the base of my neck, squeezing as her lips trace the line of my jaw. Her legs are sitting on the outside of my thighs as she rides me hard and fast.

Her hips grind against me, and the urge to reach out and hold her against me is at war within me.

As much as I want to let her take over and call the shots taking her pleasure, I also can't deny how bad I wish I could hold her and make love to her slowly.

"Ivy," I groan, reaching out to slide my hands over her thighs, helping guide her movements. She stops for a moment before she continues. All bets are off now. Reaching one hand up, I rip the wrap off my head.

Her head is thrown back as I ravage her chest. She's still dressed in her lingerie. Pulling her top down, I grab her breast in my hand, taking her nipple in my mouth, sucking hard.

"Oh, God." She snakes her arms around my neck while she continues to ride me. Grabbing her by her thighs, I lift her into my arms, tightening her legs around my waist, carrying her over to the bed.

Setting her down on the edge, I carefully slide off her heels, letting them fall on the floor as I pull her nightie over her head. I follow her as she climbs up the bed. Moving her leg over my shoulder, I line my dick up with her center, brushing the tip over her pussy.

"Does that feel good?"

She nods as she throws her head back, opening her legs wider for me as I enter her slowly. Just the head at first, before pulling all the way out and then taking her hard and fast.

Moving both of her thighs over my shoulders, I bend her body back as I fuck her. We move like that, chasing our orgasms before she slides her legs down around my waist.

Pinning her down between my arms, I press a deep kiss against her lips. I don't know what it is about this kiss, but it feels different. It doesn't feel like it's just Brix and Ivy; now it's like there's something more there. Something deeper.

My movements slow, as her fingers dig into my lower back, holding me to her as I thrust in and out. Easing up, I peer down at her, her eyes bright as she stares up at me.

"I love you, Ivy," I murmur, with every ounce of love left in me.

Unshed tears fill her eyes as she grabs my neck, pulling me in close to her again.

"I want you to cum with me."

Ivy's hand slides down between us, her fingers moving with urgency as she brushes over her swollen bud down her pussy lips to wrap around my dick then back up again. Each time she brushes over her clit, her grip on my dick tightens.

"Oh, God, baby."

"I'm coming," she moans, her walls and legs both tighten around me. Thrusting deep once more, I collapse next to her, pulling her with me to press her back against my chest. Every ounce of energy I have drains out of me.

I don't even remember falling asleep, exhaustion sinking in and swallowing me whole. A little while later, I jostle, expecting to find Ivy with her body melded against mine.

Lifting my head off the pillow, I look around for any sign of her, my arm reaching out to pat the empty bed next to me.

"Ivy?" I yell out.

The music and the lights overhead are both off now, enveloping the room in silence and darkness.

Swinging my legs over the side of the mattress, I feel around for my pants near the chair and pull on my briefs. I check the bathroom first, expecting to find her there, but when the light is off, a knot in my stomach coils.

"Ivy?" I shout.

Pushing the door open to her room, I search, hoping maybe she came back in here. Her closet door is open, and I immediately notice all of her clothes that once hung there are now gone.

It takes me a second to register what I'm seeing as I flick the light on. I pull the drawers to her dresser open, looking for some missing clue as to what is going on. My eyes are frantic, looking for some sort of explanation for where she went and why all her clothes are missing.

"Ivy!" I holler, louder this time as I race into the hallway, peering over the balcony to the living room.

The only other place I would expect to see her, on the couch, is empty as well.

Turning back around to head to my room for my phone, something on her bed catches my eye. I hadn't noticed it at first, but it looks like a note.

I nearly trip as I run toward it, panic-stricken.

Picking up the envelope, red lips cover the back over the seal. My fingers brush over the kiss as I tear it open pulling out the notecard.

Joke's on you

What? Joke's on me?

My knees hit the floor as the world around me spins.

She knows. She found out, and she left.

Pushing myself to my feet, I sprint down the stairs toward the front door. As I open the large, wood door, stepping out onto the stoop, I call out her name over and over.

Her car is gone.

Ivy is gone.

Ivy is gone.

I repeat the words over and over as I fall back, sitting in the doorway, running my hands through my hair, staring down at the note in my hand.

She found out about the bet.

Tonight, I told her I loved her.

She left.

The joke's on me.

CHAPTER TWENTY-FIVE

BRIX

"Hi, my name is Brix. I'm here for Tamara Ward."

"Yes, Ms. Tamara has been looking forward to seeing you. If you want to have a seat, she will be out in just a few minutes."

I eye the row of chairs lining the wall. They are hard and dingy, but hopefully, I won't be waiting for too long.

It feels like I've waited for this day for much longer than sixty days. When my mom was admitted into rehab, I wasn't sure what the other end of her time here would look like.

Over the course of the past two months, I've been here a few times to meet with her and her counselor. One of the steps to her going back home is to understand who she'll be around and what her new life will look like.

We decided it is best she move in with my Uncle Travis. While he does have my niece staying with him, he shares custody with his ex, and she would be able to help her.

Things have moved fast for me and the guys. We recently met with Lights Off Records and they've offered us a record deal. It's a huge break for us, and if all goes well, we'll have our own album coming out next year.

The last few months have been hell, though. Since Ivy left, I haven't felt like myself. Well, at least the man I was when we were together. She won't talk to me, not that I can blame her. I've been the one who has written most of our music up until this point, and ever since she left, I can't bring myself to write a word. The guys and our label have been pressuring me to get something done.

I've been able to hold them off so far, telling them things with my mom have taken up most of my thoughts.

Which isn't a lie.

The full truth is I can't even connect with anything I write. My mind and my heart aren't in it. I'm on the brink of getting everything we've worked so hard for, and all I can think about is Ivy.

"Brix." I hear my mom's voice filter through the room.

Tears sting my eyes at the sound of her voice. Every time I hear her talk, her words clear, brings me back to when I was younger. I don't even remember the last time I heard my mom speak to me sober.

The thought reaches into my chest, wrapping itself around my heart with a vise grip.

"Mom," I murmur, standing as she wraps her arms around me.

She even smells like her, like she did before. Like lavender, only now it's mixed in with the sterile scent of this place.

"It's so good to see you, honey."

"You, too, Mom."

She pulls back, tears filling her eyes. She reaches her hand out, pressing her palm against my cheek as she flashes me her warm smile.

"Don't cry." I pull her in, giving her another hug. "You're too pretty to cry, Ma. It's okay."

"It's more than okay," she sighs, her arms wrapped tightly around me.

She's come a long way, and I'm so ready to take her home.

"You got your stuff?" I ask as she steps back.

I spot the duffel bag a few feet behind her, having dropped it when she stepped out in the hallway. Brushing her fingers beneath her eyes, she wipes her tears, before bending down to pick up her bag.

I recognize Clint, the director, standing behind her with a smile on his face.

"You ready, Tamara?"

"Yes." She smiles. Her confidence in just one word fills me with so much hope. While it won't always be easy, she's in a much better place mentally than she's ever been.

"We'll see you this Wednesday for group. Have a good weekend."

He folds his hands in front of him as we pass by and out the door.

The moment the sun hits my mom's face, she pauses and takes a deep breath.

"I forgot how much I love stopping to enjoy the fresh air."

"Well, we'll have to drive back to town with the windows down then."

We used to go for drives with the windows down and the music turned up growing up. It's how my love of music first began, sitting in the back of her old station wagon with Willie Nelson and Johnny Cash playing on the stereo.

Lifting her bag into the back of my truck, I hold the door open for her while she climbs into the passenger seat.

"I'll even let you pick the radio station." I grin, slipping the key in the ignition.

"Wow. I feel really special now." She laughs. "Go ahead and play whatever you want, sweetie."

I opt to start with a song from a playlist I know she'll like. As soon as the song starts playing, she closes her eyes, tilting her head back against the headrest.

We don't talk for most of the ride back to town, choosing to sit in the comfortable silence mixed with music playing. When we start approaching the outskirts of Carolina Beach, she reaches forward to turn the knob lowering the volume.

"How have you been, honey?"

"Good." I hope the response doesn't sound as forced as it felt.

"Your Uncle Travis told me about your record deal. I'm so proud of you, Brix. You know that?"

"I do," I reply honestly.

"What's on your mind?"

"What? Nothing."

"Don't lie to me. I'm your mom, I know when you're not yourself. You seem sad."

I hate how she can tell, and I immediately feel guilty. I don't want her to think this has anything to do with her.

"I'm fi—"

"Brix," she cuts me off. "Please don't hold back talking to me as some way of protecting me from your problems. You don't need to shelter me or handle me with kid gloves. Let me be there for you for a change."

"It's really nothing, Mom. I promise."

"What's her name?"

My eyes dart over to hers, taken by surprise. She smiles, realizing she's right as she looks back out the window.

Before the divorce, before the drinking, she could always tell when I was lying. When I was up to no good, she could always see past all the bullshit.

"Ivyana." It feels weird saying her full name out loud to anyone but her. I had always called her Ivy, but in a way, the woman I met and fell in love with wasn't the same girl I knew back then.

Except, whenever I thought about calling her Ivyana, I always felt like I was somehow separating them. Like I was choosing to forget the girl I used to give a hard time, whose life I made miserable.

I felt like an asshole not acknowledging they were the same person, so I forced myself to continue to call her Ivy, even though I loved her full name.

"That's a beautiful name."

"She's beautiful." My voice comes to life with those words.

"What happened?"

"I fucked it up." I laugh. Pulling my hat off, I rake my fingers through my hair, pulling on the strands before tugging my hat back on.

"Do you love her?"

The question takes me by surprise. My mind immediately goes back to that night, telling her how I felt about her, only to wake up to find her gone.

To be honest, I love her more than anything in this world. Even knowing that, I don't blame her for leaving. She deserves far more than anything I could ever give her, even if I could somehow manage to convince her how sorry I am.

I've tried reaching out to her a few times in the past few weeks, but when the calls started getting sent to voice mail, I stopped.

She deserves to move on without me bothering her. It isn't because I stopped caring or she isn't worth fighting for. It is the exact opposite.

It doesn't mean I haven't kept up with how she is doing. I manage to prove to Kyla I'm not a complete scumbag, and she's filled me in on how she's been.

Despite finding the note on her bed, I knew better than to think what we felt between us was a joke. If anything, the only joke was either of us thinking we weren't in this deeper than we tried to play it off to be.

"I do," answering her earlier question.

"Then, I don't care what you did, if you love her, she deserves for you to fight for her."

Pulling up in front of Travis's house, I put the car in park and look over at my mom.

"I don't know if there are enough words in the English language that could prove to her how sorry I am."

A small smile lines the curve of her lips as she reaches out, grabbing my hand. "Don't tell her then, Brix. Show her."

She opens the door, stepping out and shutting it behind her. She picks up the bag from the back of the truck as she comes around to my side. Leaning over, she folds her arms on the windowsill.

"I love the man you are, Brix. I think if you showed her more of him, she'd know the kind of person you truly are. She wouldn't be able to help loving you back. Thank you for the ride."

She ducks her head into the truck, kissing me on my cheek before pulling back, picking up her bag, and walking up the driveway.

Travis is standing at the door, holding it open for her as he waves me off. I feel bad for not staying longer, having to head over to Tysin's house to meet up with the guys. We loaded up our stuff earlier today, so I could be there when my mom was released.

Flipping the song on my playlist, I lean forward, hitting the dial, turning up the music. Even with the music blaring trying to drown out my thoughts, the sound of my mom's words plays over and over in my head.

Don't tell her, Brix. Show her.

How would I even begin to prove to Ivy how much she means to me? How do you show someone you've hurt how important they are to you?

I may not have any idea, but I'm going to give it a try.

I only hope she'll give me a chance.

CHAPTER TWENTY-SIX

IVY

It didn't take long before news spread I left town and the reasons why. I sent a quick text to Jayde when I stopped at the gas station, apologizing, and explained something came up and I had to leave. I felt terrible leaving the way I did, but I couldn't face staying there any longer. She seemed to know the news before I told her.

Brix blew up my phone with calls and texts the next day, to the point I turned off my phone. I knew he wasn't taking it well, but honestly, I had nothing more left to say to him. He kept trying to reach out to me for the first couple of days, but I wasn't ready to talk to him, wasn't sure if I ever would be.

The calls and texts stopped, and sooner or later, it seemed like it was all a dream. Except, it wasn't, the memories were still there holding me captive.

It made it hard to focus. Everywhere I went, it seemed like something was popping up, reminding me of him. Thankfully, school kept me busy and my mind occupied.

When I wasn't busy with school, I was making plans with Kyla to come down to visit or hitting up the clubs with my roommate, Hensley. Those nights were the hardest, and I'd prefer to stay home, watching Netflix.

Every band we'd go out to see play ended up reminding me of Brix in one way or another. I'd stand there, lost in a daze thinking about him. Which brings me to tonight...

"Did she say when she'd be here?" Hensley questions, huddled up against the side of the brick wall outside of Vibrate.

The temperatures have dropped with the cooler weather. We're both dressed for dancing, which isn't doing us any favors right now.

"Yeah, she just texted me a few minutes ago saying she was pulling into the parkade. She should be here any second."

"Okay, good!" she huffs. "'Cause it's frickin' cold out here."

We've been counting down the days to this show for a month when Kyla scored us tickets to see High Octane. They are hands down one of my favorite bands, and I've been dying to see them live.

We don't normally make a habit of hitting up Vibrate. She's convinced you'll see the type of guys you'd find on Wall Street down here. Although, we both know High Octane is bringing in more of my type of men.

Hensley wants to find herself an investment banker who has his shit together and can take care of her in more ways than one.

As for me, I'm still struggling to get Brix out of my mind. I've heard him play High Octane on several occasions. In fact, the night he was bangin' blondie in the room next to me, one of the songs playing was theirs.

Every time I thought of coming here tonight, my mind kept circling back to him. To the conversation I had with Kyla when I came back to school; how he was losing his mind over me leaving.

Whenever I think about why he was upset, I've come up with several different reasons. I've analyzed and dissected every scenario, but I always find myself back to the very first night I returned to Carolina Beach.

The night I first went to Whiskey Barrel and watched them playing, the night he hit on me and asked me out. Knowing him like I do now, I know he was pissed when I turned him down.

When has Brix Ward ever been told no?

The only conclusion I can come up with as to why he was so upset was because, for once, he was treated like what was going on between us meant nothing to me.

He let me be the fool, leading me to believe he wanted to be with me.

Joke's on him.

"Hey, girl, heyy," Kyla sings as she runs toward us. She's dressed in a sexy, short red dress and high heels. So high I'm staring at her with wide eyes, begging her to stop before she breaks her ankle.

"Dude, Ivy, you look sexy as hell."

She stops, eyeing me in my little black dress before zoning in on my new ivy tattoo through my sheer tights, starting on my calf wrapped up around my thigh. It's chilly tonight, so I opted for my favorite pair with bows on the back of my legs, pairing them with my black heels.

Snaking my arm around her neck, I pull her in for a hug.

"I missed you," I whisper in her ear, her arms tightening around my lower back.

"I missed you more."

"This is Hensley. Hensley, this is Kyla." I hold my hand out, introducing my two friends. They've spoken to each other over the phone, but this is the first time they've ever met in person.

"I feel like I've known you forever." Hensley laughs, hugging Kyla before we head over to join the long line wrapped around the side of the building.

I check the time on the phone. We have about ten minutes before the opening band goes on.

"He's gonna go crazy when he sees her."

Glancing behind me, for a second, I thought I heard Kyla talking. She's looking innocently between me and Hensley.

"Did you say something?"

"No, I think it was someone else behind us."

She plasters a fake smile on her face, but I'm not buying it.

"Good try. What did you say?"

"I swear it wasn't me. Someone back there was saying how their parents were going to go crazy when they found out they got a parking ticket or something."

"A parking ticket?"

"Yep." Kyla grins. "Parking here is a pain in the ass. You really should move back to CB."

Rolling my eyes, I turn back around to find there's like five feet between us and the group in front of us as we walk to rejoin the rest of the line. We don't have to wait too much longer before our tickets are scanned and we head inside to find our seats.

"I'm so excited!" I shout, as we slip through the crowd of people to find our seats.

Kyla was able to score some incredible tickets, so we aren't too far from the stage. Third row, right in the center.

Just as we make it to our spot, the lights go dim. The only lights are the ones circling the crowd like spotlights. The sound of drums kicks in, pounding a heavy beat, kickstarting the adrenaline coursing through me.

The crowd starts to cheer as I clap my hands. The guitar joins in as the neon-blue lights highlight the stage before focusing on the sign on the wall behind the drummer illuminating the name A Rebels Havoc.

My body goes rigid, my hands running absentmindedly over my arms. A spotlight begins to circle overhead as Tysin walks out, the guitar resting against his hip. One strum over the strings sends the crowd into a frenzy.

I search for any sign of Brix. When his voice filters through the speakers around us, I close my eyes to hold back the tears that threaten to fill my eyes at hearing his voice again.

My heart is beating in double-time to the drums, it feels like it is about to pound right out of my chest.

"How the fuck are we?" he bellows.

My eyes turn, falling on Kyla, tears filling her eyes as she gives me a sad smile.

"The parking here really is fucking terrible though."

Shaking my head, she wraps her arms around my waist once again. This time, I feel like I'm holding her in hopes she'll keep me stable because I'm not sure I'm ready for what tonight's going to bring.

"It's going to be okay," she reassures me. She swipes her finger at the lone tear that escaped and is now rolling down my face.

"I hope so," I mouth to her. Her hand finds mine, squeezing it quickly as we turn back to the stage.

"We're A Rebels Havoc. If you haven't heard of us, well it's time you fuckin' fix that."

I can't help but want to smile listening to him.

They play a few songs, ones I know from my time back at Whiskey Barrel. It dawns on me while Brix feeds into the crowd, drawing out their cheers, he hasn't gone back to performing the way he did the first night I watched them.

I sing along with them as he plays. Multiple times I wonder if Brix is able to see me, his eyes squinting as he searches the crowd, but if he does, he doesn't give anything away.

"Thank you for letting us be here tonight to open for High Octane. Before we head out, I want to play one last song. If you're a fan of our music, this one will be new to you. Somethin' I've been working on for the past couple weeks. If it's cool with you, I'd like to see what ya think."

Brix turns back toward Madden, holding his hand up to signal something, as Tysin starts to play.

"Ivy," Brix says, pausing. "This one's for you."

This time the guitar leads with the intro as Brix nods his head along to the beat of the music, staring down at the floor.

With my hand balled into a fist, I press it against my mouth, watching in awe as they begin to play.

The song is slower than their others. When Brix's voice joins in, I almost don't recognize him. The words are soft and filled with so much emotion. I find myself absorbed in his performance, truly listening to the lyrics of the song, the timbre of his voice. My breath hitches, caught in my throat as he sings about needing me, how he would give anything to have me back, and how losing me broke him.

If he hadn't had said the song was for me in the beginning, all questions would've gone away as he weaves my name into the lyrics, as he speaks about a woman wrapping herself around him and his heart.

The beat of the song is catchy, and while the crowd around us sways to the music, I stand frozen in place, soaking up every second of the words and the ache of his voice as he sings.

Thinking back to all those nights I'd lie awake in my bed, thinking about why he was upset when I left, it is like I know now. I can feel the pain he is feeling. His eyes are closed, his hand clenched in a fist against his heart.

When the song is over, I feel the ache in my chest, the same empty feeling I had felt for weeks missing him.

"Oh my God," Hensley whispers next to me, her arm banded around me as she leans in close to check on me.

"Are you okay?"

"I think so," I murmur, forcing myself to push aside all the emotions building inside.

I tried to enjoy the rest of the night, knowing I had been looking forward to High Octane's concert, but no matter how hard I tried, I couldn't stop thinking of Brix.

I was zoned out, replaying the song on a loop, over and over in my head.

When the concert was over, all I could think about was trying to find a way to get backstage so I could see him.

"Kyla!" I shout over the crowd of people as we sidestep our way out of our row of seating.

"Don't worry. He has a backstage pass waiting for you up front. C'mon!"

We find our way to the front. The crowd of people is thick. Navigating our way seems to take hours. The spike of anxiety at seeing him has adrenaline pumping through me.

As soon as we round the corner toward the admissions box, I spot him standing against the wall. His head is covered with a black baseball cap sitting low on his head, but I'd know him anywhere.

Two large security guards flank him on both sides as I cut across the room, making a beeline for him.

"Ivy!" Kyla shouts from behind me. The sound of my name being called has him raising his head, and his eyes meet mine.

I halt my movement as he pushes off the wall, taking a step closer to me. Biting my lip, I'm suddenly unsure of what to say or if this is even a good idea.

I don't know what I'm doing anymore.

CHAPTER TWENTY-SEVEN

BRIX

I prayed like hell Kyla was able to pull through and convince Ivy to come. When I told her what I had planned, I begged her to do whatever she could to get her here.

I even took care of getting her the tickets.

The lighting in the club didn't compare to other venues we had played lately, so it was hard to see her in the crowd, but I hoped she was there, listening.

After the concert was over, I took off back to the dressing room to shower, leaving the guys to watch High Octane's performance.

Things have been getting better between me and the guys. After Ivy left, I had a few choice words for Tysin, accusing him of telling her about the bet before I had a chance to come clean.

At the end of the day, regardless of how Tysin had egged it on, it was my mistake. I made the choice of saying what I said, letting him get to me when he was trying to get a rise out of me.

I ended up doing something stupid and hurt someone who means the world to me in the process. If she gave me a chance to talk to her, to explain, I'd spend the rest of my life proving to her how much I love her.

Standing against the brick wall, I watch as the crowd filters out of the building. Pulling the baseball cap down low on my head, I try to keep a low profile, not wanting any attention right now.

I am only out here in hopes of finding Ivy. Security wouldn't let them through from the stage, so I know this is the only way she'll get back to where I am.

"Ivy!" I hear shouted over the crowd of people shuffling out the door toward the main exit.

Looking up, my eyes immediately fall on her, and fuck me, my heart nearly stops in my chest from the sight of her. Ivy is beautiful, but something about looking at her now, coming to terms with my feelings for her, has made her even more gorgeous.

"Hey," I say, pushing off the wall, approaching the gates.

"Hi." She smiles shyly.

My eyes break away from hers, taking in the sexy-as-sin dress she's wearing, down to her black tights covering her legs.

I've always had a special love for Ivy's legs. Fuck, they've been the center of many sexual dreams. Not even my memory or the thoughts I've dreamt up in my mind compare to seeing them in person, but I pause when I see the intricate design wrapped around her leg.

"Did you mean it?"

Confused as to what she could mean, I narrow my eyes in question.

"The song. The lyrics. Did you mean it?"

"Yes," I reply, matter-of-factly.

Reaching my hand out for hers, she hesitates, staring at it before looking back up to me. I hate how she's even second-guessing it, but before I'm able to say anything, she places her hand in mine.

Leading her through the gates, she stops to look back at Kyla and a blonde girl I don't know or recognize.

"Hens, will you wait for me for a few minutes?"

"Yeah, no problem. I'll go grab my car. Once the crowd dies down, I'll meet you out front."

"Actually, if you don't mind, I'll just give her a lift home."

Ivy turns back at me, her eyes roaming over my face, smiling once again before she turns back to her friend.

"Is that okay?"

"Of course." She grins. They both turn to leave, as her friend stops and turns back to face me. Stone-faced, she says, "If you ever hurt her again, I'll have your dick cut off and shoved down your throat."

Gaping at her, I cough out a laugh. Her jaw clenches, clearly not liking my response, as I wipe it off my face.

"I'll do you one better. If I ever hurt Ivy like that again, I'll personally hand you the knife."

She grins. "Good answer."

"Bye." Ivy smiles, waving at her friends before turning back to me.

The hesitant look she wore before is gone.

Rubbing my thumb over the soft skin on the back of her hand, I pull her in closer to me, wrapping her arm around mine. I'm not usually one to be overly affectionate with women unless it's leading up to going to bed together. This is different. My body has felt the loss of not having her close to me for too long. I crave the feel of her soft skin, the weight of her body pressed against mine.

"This is my dressing room. I hoped you'd be here tonight, so I asked for a separate space. I wanted us to have somewhere to go to talk before we had to leave."

I shut and lock the door behind us, not wanting to be interrupted by anyone. Guiding her over to the couch on the back wall of the room, I take a seat, pulling her to sit on my lap.

"God, I've missed you so fucking much," I whisper, pressing a soft kiss against her shoulder.

Goose bumps spread over her skin sending shivers through her. I love how her body still seems to respond to my touch.

"I have so much I want to say, but I want to sit here with you. I want to forget all the problems we've had between us. As much as I know we need to talk about them, I also don't want to drudge it all up again."

"Well, we can't pretend like it didn't happen." Her words come out bitter, anger seeping into her tone.

"Of course not, but aren't I allowed to want to be around you for a few minutes before I have to see the hurt in your eyes knowing I'm the one who put it there? Fuck, Ivy. Do you seriously think this has been easy for me? Do you really believe this is what I want?"

"Actually, yes, I do. Did anyone hold a gun to your head? Were you forced to make a bet with Tysin with the end goal of breaking my heart?"

"No..."

"Then what makes you think I'm going to believe you? Is this some part of your prank still? To pull me in here, show me some sad, puppy dog looks in your eyes in hopes I'll forgive you and you can get back at me? Make me pay for being the one who gave you a dose of your own medicine?"

She pushes my hands away from her as she moves to stand.

"What? No, Ivy. Dammit, I can explain. Just give me a chance to explain."

Standing, she crosses her arms in front of her. I want to lean forward, wrap my fingers in hers, and pull her back to me. Tell her to give me a chance, and I will, but before I start, I want her in my arms again.

There's a time to give her space and a time to push her further, pull her closer to me even if she says it's not what she wants. This isn't one of those times.

She wants her space, and the last thing I want is to piss her off even more than I already have.

I take my hat off, tossing it to the side somewhere so I can see her better.

Taking a heavy breath, I begin, "It started the night you started working at Whiskey Barrel. Tysin was giving me shit about you turning me down."

Her eyes narrow as she rocks back and forth on her heels, waiting for me to continue.

"Ivy... fuck. Will you promise me no matter what I say that you'll stay here and let me explain?"

She keeps clenching her hands into fists, before ringing them out as she bites her lip. I hate thinking about the pain this is causing her.

"Please. Just promise me."

"I promise, Brix. Now tell me already."

There's an urgency, frustration in her voice. It's different than how she's ever talked to me before, and I hate that I'm the cause of it right now.

"Anyway..." I lean forward, rubbing my fingers over my forehead, massaging them into my skin.

"Tysin was starting shit with me after the show ended, and I said something about if the girls were single, to hit me up or whatever. I knew you were there, that you were listening. I shouldn't have let him bother me, but I did.

"He kept razzing me about how you rejected me, saying I cared more than I wanted to believe. He wasn't wrong, but things with us, in the beginning, had been so volatile, I wasn't about to admit it.

"He kept talking about what you think of me, and I don't know, I just snapped. I told him I could get you to change your mind. That I'd have you eating out of the palm of my hand by the end of the summer."

I pause, staring at the floor and Ivy's feet as she paces from side to side in her high heels. I'm stalling while I muster up the courage to tell her the last of it, but I don't even know how. This could ruin every chance we may have to get back together. But if she finds out I'm lying now, it'll be hell to pay when she learns the truth.

"I told him I hated you, just like I had back then. That I'd fuck you, then I'd send you back to school heartbroken."

My voice cracks as I utter the last words. Tears fill to the brim of her eyes as she closes them. Her mouth falls open, trying to slow her breathing. I tell myself it's going to be okay, but in the back of my mind, I wonder if she's preparing herself to leave. If the reason why she closed her eyes is because she can't bear the sight of me.

The tears that once filled her eyes, now stream down her beautiful face. I'm fighting against myself to sit here and wait, but all I want to do is pull her into my arms and hold her.

"Can I please touch you?"

I don't even care if I sound like I'm begging because I am, and I would.

She opens her eyes, looking down at me. Her stare is void of any emotion, and I wonder if I broke her.

I wait for any response before she snaps out of it and takes a step toward me. When she does, I grab her hand, guiding her into my lap. She doesn't resist, and I'm relieved as she sits, stretching her legs out in front of her on the other side of the couch.

"I need you to know everything I said to you after you came back home that night down by the beach was real. I had planned to tell you everything when we stayed at the beach house. I wanted a chance somewhere away from everything to come clean, but when you told me your fears, how you were still scared to give in, I knew it wasn't the right time. I needed to show you how I felt about you, I needed you to believe me when I told you I loved you. It's just, there's never a good time to sit the person you love down and tell them the things you know will break their heart. I'm sorry though, for not telling you sooner. Hell, I'm sorry I made the bet in the first place, but I'd never want to hurt you. Never! Do you know how much it gutted me when I found out you left?"

I wrap my arms around her waist, holding onto her, not wanting to let her go. She relaxes a little more. I stare at her as she traces the collar of my shirt, hoping she'll look at me. I want to kiss her so damn bad, but I'm trying like hell to prove this isn't about wanting to get in her pants, even though seeing her tonight, being near her, touching her is driving me out of my damn mind.

"So much good has happened to me since you came back into my life, with a smart mouth full of sass. The guys and I were offered a record deal. For the first time ever, I've found someone, besides my mom, who means more to me than my own life. I've been a selfish asshole for the last twenty-three years, but it's different with you. I want you next to me when we release our first single when our record comes out. I want you with me when we go on tour. I know I've given you every reason not to trust me, to run away, but please, give me a chance."

"A chance for what? Brix, do you really think we'd be able to do long-distance when you're out traveling for shows, or when you go on the road? I mean, look at us. We've spent more time fighting with each other than anything at all."

I grin. "We are good at fighting, yes. But think of all the fun we'll have making up."

She smacks me on the chest, pushing me away, as my hold on her tightens. She shakes her head, and in the mirror in front of us, I can see her rolling her eyes before a subtle grin lines her mouth.

"We'll figure it out. We can FaceTime every night. I'll make plans to come see you as often as I can. You graduate in what five, six months?"

She nods, turning to look down at me.

"Ivy, do you love me?"

Her face softens. My breath is caught in my throat, waiting for her to answer as she nods her head once again.

"Tell me," I whisper.

"I love you, Brix."

Wrapping my hand around the back of her head, I kiss her. I kiss her like she's the air I need to breathe, like she's the blood pumping through my veins, and the heart beating in my chest. Like she's the only thing in this world that means anything to me, and I hope like hell she feels it, too.

Pulling back, I press our foreheads together and whisper, "I love you, too. I promise I'll never let you forget how much."

Tears fill her eyes once again as I kiss her. This time softly, as she quickly moves to stand and climbs back on top of me, facing me.

My hands roam over her body, her thighs, over her waist up toward her chest, sliding back down to her hips to pull her closer to me. It's been too long since I've been near her.

I'm going to show her how much I've been missing her.

CHAPTER TWENTY-EIGHT

BRIX

SIX MONTHS LATER

"Do you see her?" Charlene leans closer to ask.

Looking down from the stands into the crowd of graduates, my eyes roam for any sight of my girl. She's hard to spot in a sea of people wearing the same cap and gown, but I know if I spot her, I'll know it's her.

"There she is," I say, pointing, as Ivy looks up at us. Even from here, I can see the smile beaming on her face as she takes a seat.

Today's the day we've been waiting for. The last six months haven't always been easy, especially the last couple of weeks with things getting busy for the band. We've had to do a lot more traveling as we've been working on our record.

It's cut into my time to see Ivy, but she's been so reassuring. There hasn't been a night where we've gone to bed without speaking to each other. Most nights we FaceTime when I'm back in my room away from everyone else.

On the nights when the ache of not being near her stings the most, I love her in only the way I can being far away. Watching her touch herself for me, letting me see her in the most intimate of moments. Fuck, I don't know how I got so lucky with this girl.

Now, she's finally graduating, and I won't have to be away from her as long. I told the label I had to leave to come back to North Carolina this week to see her. There's no way I was going to miss seeing her graduate. She's been there for me every step of the way since we got back together, and I wasn't going to miss this milestone for her.

Sitting next to her mom, hearing them say her name, and watching her walk across the stage is one of my proudest moments. Standing, I stick two fingers in my mouth, whistling as she stops in the middle of the stage to look up at me. I can see the smile on her face as she reaches her hand up to blow me a kiss.

After the ceremony is over, I walk with Charlene down the stairs toward the front of the event center waiting for Ivy to join us. It reminds me of the same night we had not too long ago when I waited for her to come walking out of Vibrate, the night we got back together.

"I'm so proud of you, honey," Charlene says, as Ivy finds us, shuffling through the crowd of people.

She wraps her arms around her, whispering something in her ear as Ivy stares at me over her shoulder.

I wink at her, earning me another one of those beautiful smiles.

It wasn't long after Ivy and I got back together that Charlene and my father's divorce was filed and finalized.

I hated to say it when I found out they eloped, but it was inevitable. Jasper Ward is a selfish man. Hell, where do you think I got it? He's never been faithful to any woman he's been with, and I'm glad Charlene got out before she was in deep like my mother.

She seems to be doing well, though. After they separated, she made the move to Chapel Hill where Ivy went to school. She wanted a fresh start and being close to Ivy again was good for both of them.

Charlene moves to take a step back, as Ivy steps in close to me. Pulling her in my arms, I press my face in her hair, kissing her.

"I'm proud of you, too, baby."

"Thank you."

Whispering low enough for only her to hear me, "All I keep thinking about is how beautiful you look. Wear that cap and those heels for me later tonight, please."

"You would, Ward." She laughs, pushing back at me.

My face turns serious. "Ivyana Marie."

There's a heat that passes over her face when I call her by her full name. She doesn't say anything, simply nods. I press my lips together, firmly, and shove my hands in my pockets to resist pulling her out of here, in front of her mother and finding us somewhere private.

She knows it, too, as she looks at my arms and the fists bulging in the pockets of my pants, biting down on her lip to hold back her smile.

We join her mom for dinner before we hit the road. It's late by the time we make it to Myrtle Beach, staying at the beach house for the weekend.

Ivy's sitting in the middle of the bench seat of my pickup, her head on my shoulder, sleeping.

"Wake up, baby. We're here."

She lifts her head, looking up at me as I kiss her softly. Reaching over, her hand grips the front of my t-shirt, deepening it. Our tongues tangle together, and I almost forget we're sitting in the middle of the open driveway, where the neighbors not too far could likely see us.

"Let's get you inside, and we can finish where this is going."

She grins, nodding as she slides over to my side and climbs out behind me.

I pick up both of our bags from the back of my truck as she grabs the keys from my pocket, heading toward the front door. I haven't been back here since we were here last summer. I thought about coming back after she left, wanting to get away, but I couldn't without her.

She flips the lights on as I set our bags down by the door. We both look around the room as she spins on her heel, looking up at me.

Raising my eyebrow suggestively, her body molding against mine as my hands roam over her sides, reaching for the back of her thighs to pick her up. Her legs wrap around my waist, rubbing against me in the most deliciously torturous way possible.

I walk with her like that through the entryway and into the dining room, setting her on the edge of the counter. Her arms are band around my neck, holding me against her as her mouth ravages me.

It's been two weeks since we've been together, and my body is on overdrive wanting to feel her again. Her hand slips between us, reaching for my belt.

I want to help her, to speed this process along, but when she finally gets the belt through the loop and tugs my zipper down, her hand quickly finds its way home wrapped around me. I have to lock my knees in order to keep myself standing because the feel of her soft, warm hand stroking me has my eyes rolling back in my head.

"Fuuuuuuck." She presses a kiss against my lips, hard and full of passion.

Reaching my hands up, I twist my fingers into her long, curly hair holding her mouth against mine. My breathing comes out ragged, struggling through every move she makes.

None of those FaceTime dates compare to feeling her body against mine.

She pulls back, lifting her palm in front of her mouth as she spits on it before she resumes touching me.

"You dirty girl," I moan, feeling her hand slide over me.

My hips thrust into her palm, wanting more.

"I need to feel you, baby." My hands find their way to her waist, unbuttoning her pants. She's still wearing those sexy heels she had on during her graduation ceremony and a pair of trouser shorts, along with this sexy, lace top.

She looks so fucking good, I'm not sure if I want her to wear the top or if I want to rip it off her.

Slipping her shoes off her feet, I slide her pants down her legs. My eyes zero in on the red thong she's wearing as a guttural groan slips out of my mouth.

Wrapping my hand around my dick, I hold her off, trying not to cum as I bend down. She knows exactly what I'm after, as she spreads her legs open for me. I use my other hand to trace the edge of her panties, down toward her pussy, sliding the material to the side.

She's wet, glistening under the bright light as she falls back against the cabinets.

"Touch me," she begs.

"Where?"

"You know where, Brix. Quit teasing me."

"Oh, baby, I could tease you all night if I wanted to. Tell me where."

"My fucking pussy, Brix. I want your tongue on my fucking clit. Now."

"Mm... there she is. As you wish."

Leaning in closer, I pull the edge of her panties to the side as I press the tip of my tongue against her, barely tracing a line from her pussy up toward her clit. Her breaths come out in heavy pants as her fingers grip my hair, holding me close.

She pushes me closer to her, creating more friction where she wants me as she rides my face.

I moan against her as she cries out, "Oh, God" over and over.

I'm trying hard not to cum just from her sounds and the taste of her juices on my lips.

Tightening my fist, trying to hold myself off, I pull back and mutter, "Baby, let me feel you squeeze that pussy around me."

"Yes, yes." Her chest heaves with every word. She reaches down between us, holding her panties to the side.

Wrapping my hands around her hips, I pull her to the edge of the counter, tracing the head of my dick through her folds until I slide in.

"Oh. My. God." Ivy's hand reaches out for me, as I hold her hips in my hands, driving into her hard and fast. I wanted to take my time, slowly make love to her, but that'll have to come later. I can't get enough of her, enough of the feel of her pussy wrapped around me.

"Fuck, it feels so damn good."

I thrust into her twice, her moans echoing around us, I thrust once more before collapsing on top of her. Our bodies tremble, the aftermath of our release as all the energy drains out of me, and I relax into her.

"I've missed you so fucking much. Goddamn."

"I love you, too, baby." She giggles, wrapping her hands in my hair as she pulls me up to give her a kiss.

Checking the time on the microwave, it's getting late. We don't even bother grabbing our bags by the door, as I pick her up in my arms, carrying her down the hall and to the bedroom with me.

"I just wanna lie with you in my arms," I whisper, helping her out of her top as she unhooks her bra, tossing it on the floor. I pull my shirt off over my head before I climb in next to her.

We lie together, the curtains to the sliding glass door leading out onto the balcony overlooking the ocean left open with only the night sky peeking through at us.

I don't even know how much time has passed, my hands tracing her spine when she asks, "What do you think the future looks like for us?"

"Do you mean for the two of us?"

"I mean, all of it. What does the future look like to you?"

The Brix I was when she first came back into my life hadn't given much thought to what the future looked like. All I cared about was the band and me, seeing how far we could take it.

Things have changed.

"I picture going out on the road with the guys after our album is released. I think about what it would be like to have fans buying it, singing along with us in front of sold-out crowds and in venues three times the size of the ones we've been in. And I think about you, by my side through it all. I don't want any of this if I can't have you with me along the way."

My eyes find hers in the moonlight. "I dream about you finding a job that'll allow you to come with us out on the road, us starting a family, how beautiful you'll be as our child grows inside you, and what our kids will look like. Will we have a boy who is wild and rambunctious as I was?"

"Am. Present tense. You're still wild. That's never changed."

"Or will we have a little girl who's as sassy and beautiful as her mom?"

She places her palm against the side of my face, pressing a kiss against my mouth.

Rolling her over onto her back, I slide between her legs, holding my body above hers.

"I want our future the way you see it. It sounds perfect," she murmurs as I lean forward to kiss her again.

"I do, too, baby," I say, trailing kisses down her neck to her chest.

"I guess it's time we start practicing making those babies." I peer up at her, grinning. Her eyes staring down at me, piercing me before she tosses her head back, moaning as I take her nipple in my mouth.

My life will be perfect if I get to go to bed with her, like this, every night.

EPILOGUE

IVY

It's crazy how life always seems to bring you back full circle. Two years ago, I never would've thought I'd be in a relationship with Brix, much less traveling the country with him.

A few months after I graduated from college, I landed an internship working for Mayhem Magazine. As hard as it was to be away from Brix again, that year seemed to only strengthen our relationship.

When we weren't together, Brix and the guys were putting all their energy and focus into their album, which hit the Billboard Top 100 straight out of the gate. My journalism degree and my connections to Brix helped me in networking with some of the best names in the music industry.

My boss at Mayhem had me write an article for their website after following Brix and A Rebels Havoc to Twisted

Tour last summer. Twisted Tour was a rock festival in the Phoenix area. The post got so many website visits, talking about the inside scoop and one-on-one interviews with some of the biggest bands, they offered me a job as one of their journalists.

The best part is they allowed me, more like encouraged me, to go out on the road with Brix and the guys. Not only am I being paid for what I love to do, I also get to travel the world with the man I love in the process.

Bringing us full circle, we're back in Phoenix tonight, and A Rebels Havoc is headlining for their Friday night show for Twisted Tour. The tickets have been sold out since the day they were released. I know how incredible this opportunity was for the guys when they opened here a year ago. Not to mention, we'll be staying here all weekend to watch the other shows, including High Octane, the same band they opened for when we got back together.

The guys take the stage as I glance out to take a look at the crowd. A sea of people as far as my eyes can see wait in anticipation.

Madden starts them off, as the crowd cheers in excitement, then Tysin joins on the bass guitar. Brix, dressed in his signature black t-shirt and jeans, nods his head along to the beat of the music. His leg bounces, no doubt from the adrenaline coursing through him, as he introduces them, "We're A Rebels Havoc, baby. Are you ready to fuckin' rock?"

The sound of his deep voice through the speakers has me closing my eyes, momentarily thinking back to the night before when I heard the same deep voice whisper low in my ear.

Jumping and screaming, it is clear the crowd is ready.

Being here, watching the guys play, and Brix sing, it is one of those things you can't ignore. They have a natural talent and the way they work the crowd, you can't take your eyes off them.

When they wrap up their set, they tease the crowd with an encore. Then Brix turns to the side of the stage, taking me completely by surprise, he says, "Ivy, baby, will you come out here, please?"

My eyes widen for a second, hesitant, as I slip my phone into my back pocket. Glancing over at Kyla standing next to me, she grins, nodding her head toward Brix, encouraging me to go.

Brix's eyes light up, watching me as I walk toward him. I'm careful as I do, my legs feeling wobbly, with the spike of nervous energy rushing through me.

When I get closer to him, he reaches his hand out toward me as I slip my fingers in his.

"Guys, this is my girl, Ivy. Isn't she fuckin' beautiful?"

The crowd screams around me as I laugh nervously, finally looking out at them once again before my eyes lock on his.

"Yeah, I know. She's mine, though, so, men, you can back the fuck off."

Shaking my head at him, I playfully roll my eyes as he flashes me a wink.

"Ivy, I want to say thank you in front of our friends and all these people for loving me as much as you do. For helping me to see the good in me, for making me want to be a better man for you, and for making me the happiest I've ever been."

Pulling me close to him, he presses a hard kiss against my lips, before taking a step back from me once again. The moment the connection is severed, I feel the loss of him immediately.

He reaches his hand into his pocket before he kneels on one knee, holding out a diamond ring. This ring is not your typical diamond ring. It's the most stunning thing I've ever seen, and with the bright lights shining over us, I can't hold back the tears that fill my eyes before looking up at Brix.

"Marry me. Give me the future we talked about having together."

I don't even try to hold back the tears at that point. Nodding my head, I say yes without a single hesitation. I know with everything in me, I want to spend the rest of my life with him. I hold my hands out to him, wrapping my arms around his neck as his circle my waist holding me close to him.

"I love you, baby," he whispers in my ear, pulling back to kiss me once again. The cheers and screams from the audience fade into the distance as I kiss him with everything in me.

"I love you, too."

When he finally lets me go, he yells into the mic, "Hell fuckin' yeah! She said YES!"

Realizing he's still holding the ring, he grabs my hand and slides the beautiful diamond ring on my finger.

"It's beautiful," I murmur, reaching up to try and swipe at the tears still streaming down my face.

Brix kisses me again, telling me he's going to give them one last song before he comes off stage.

Kyla is a bouncing ball of energy standing on the side of the stage, as she folds me into a hug, telling me congratulations. I'm still in shock, tremors racing through me as I hold my hand out in front of me, glancing between my ring and on stage to Brix. The joy and excitement on his face as he sings makes me think of all that's yet to come in our future.

And I can't wait to go through life, every day, with him by my side.

Thank you so much for reading Brix!

Still want more Brix and Ivy? Don't worry, I'm not done with these two yet.

Turn the page to find out how you can read their bonus epilogue. Don't miss a sneak peek at another one of my favorites, Tysin, and find out what happens between him and Kyla.

I hope you enjoy!

BONUS SCENE

Dear Reader,

I hope you enjoyed Brix and Ivy's story as much as I loved writing it.

I couldn't get enough of their love and wanted to give you a glimpse into their lives, so I wrote you a sexy and heartfelt bonus epilogue exclusively for you. All you have to do is visit the link below or scan the QR code with your phone, sign up for my newsletter, and you'll get access.

www.authorbrookeobrien.com/bonus

If you want to stay up to date with my sales and new releases, you can follow me on Bookbub at: www.bookbub.com/profile/brooke-o-brien

Brooke

BOOK TWO

USA TODAY BESTSELLING AUTHOR
BROOKE O'BRIEN

CHAPTER ONE

KYLA

Of course, of all places, he wants to go to Whiskey Barrel.

I puff my lips out and release a slow exhale. Rain trickles down the window, my breath fogging the glass. A lump I've been struggling to swallow is forming in my throat.

The news reported a tropical storm hitting the East Coast, but we're only expecting to get hit with the outer bands. It's symbolic of the absolute hell of a week I've endured with finals consuming my life.

I've graduated with my college degree, so my father can finally get off my back.

He gave up on riding my older brother, Madden, a long time ago. I guess when your son is the drummer for one of the biggest rock bands on the radio, you start to let shit slide.

Warm skin brushes over my thigh, and I shift my gaze over to Canon. He tangles our fingers together, lifting our joined hands to press a soft kiss against the back of mine.

A pair of black Ray-Bans hides his eyes, despite the sun being nowhere in sight.

My gaze snaps down to his mouth when he drags his lip between his teeth. He's dressed in a black T-shirt and denim jeans, fitting him perfectly in all the right ways. His tattooed arm is stretched out, his tanned hand firmly gripping the steering wheel. He looks every bit of the rugged badass your parents want you to stay far away from.

Except my parents love him, even if it's only because of his last name.

"It's a Friday night. Wouldn't you rather take me back to your place and fuck me against the wall?"

He slides his sunglasses off and curls the edge of his lip in a smirk. His eyes narrow, and for a second, I think I may have got to him.

He whips the car into a spot in the parking lot. He reaches for the lever to the door, then glances back before pushing it open and stepping outside.

"Dammit." I huff.

My heart drops to the pit of my stomach as the door shuts. Not because of the rejection.

It's the last thing I'd ever expect from Canon. He's never given me a reason to doubt him or his love for me since we started dating last summer.

No, the twist in my stomach has everything to do with the fact I'm only a few minutes away from seeing Tysin.

Tysin Briggs is the biggest player in Carolina Beach and a recipe for heartbreak. Yet it didn't stop me from falling in love with him two years ago. The rush and the high were intoxicating, but the crash coming down left me broken in a million pieces.

The day I walked out of the hospital, I vowed to stay as far away from him as I could. We've managed to avoid each other, but I knew this day would come sooner or later.

He's my brother's best friend and bandmate. We live in the same small town. Whiskey Barrel was his hangout, where the band started out playing all their shows.

There would be no avoiding him here.

It wasn't until Canon came along that I finally began putting the pieces of my heart back together.

My relationship with Tysin, if you could even call it one, was always kept a secret. Somehow, that made it even harder to move on.

If it weren't for the memories that haunted me and the ache in my chest, I would've thought it was all a dream.

"You comin' or what?" Canon teases, snapping me from my thoughts when he opens my door.

I climb out, stepping to the side to let him close the door before he stops me, pushing me against the side of the car.

All the stress and anxiety melt away when he pulls me into him, and I slip my arms around his waist. He trails his lips from my temple, where he presses a kiss, down to my ear.

"Let's have some fun tonight, yeah? I mean, you did just graduate from college. You should be fuckin' excited, baby. You did it!"

Guilt pangs in my chest. Why am I letting thoughts of running into Tysin ruin my night when I have Canon right in front of me?

"I always have fun when I'm with you."

He grins, tilting his forehead against mine, and kisses me deeply. I slide my fingers over his chest and pull him down, gripping the back of his neck to hold him to me. He moans, the move vibrating against my hand.

"Let's go have some fun. You deserve it."

He reaches for my hand, lacing our fingers together while we walk through the parking lot. There's a shift in my mood, a noticeable weight lifting from my chest as we round the corner toward the bar. A long line wraps around the front of the building, which only happens on the nights when A Rebels Havoc plays.

"Isn't that Tysin?" Canon asks, motioning toward the side of the building.

I follow his line of sight, my eyes immediately locking on Tysin. He's leaning against the wall, his foot tucked under him.

So much has changed since the last time I saw him. Even the way he stares at me now. The once heated look of desire is now replaced with a bitter coldness.

I know, without a doubt, he sees me, his eyes falling on where our hands are linked together.

I grit my teeth, knowing it won't be as easy to avoid him as I hoped.

He lifts his cigarette to his mouth, taking a deep inhale. His eyes eventually drag from me over to Canon before releasing a slow puff of smoke.

He's wearing a pair of black denim jeans and a red T-shirt with matching scuffed-up Vans.

I hate him for how deliciously sexy he still is, even after all this time.

It dawns on me that Canon asked me a question. Turning to find his eyes burning into the side of my face, I nod, responding with a clipped, "Yep."

When I turn my gaze forward, I notice Tysin's eyes are back on me, slowly raking over my body.

The bouncer near the front recognizes me and nods, waving me past him.

"Didn't expect to see you tonight." Tysin's deep voice grumbles as we pass by. "I thought I ran you out of here a long time ago."

My footsteps falter, and it takes everything in me not to give him a piece of my mind. It's what he wants, though. If I let him get under my skin, and he knew how much it bothers me, we'd be back to the same old cat and mouse games he likes to play.

"What was that about?" Canon questions. He looks at me, then back over at him, his brows deepening in confusion.

"Who knows?" I reply, trying to brush him off.

Meanwhile, the lump forming in my throat grows, making it impossible to ignore.

Whiskey Barrel is packed wall to wall with people. I overhear one of the bouncers tell Canon they've hit capacity, meaning they can't let anyone else enter. Carolina Beach has always turned up for their hometown heroes, and to this town, the guys of A Rebels Havoc are like gods.

It's exactly why I want to get out of here.

Canon's hand finds mine again as we make our way through the crowd of people toward the bar. The band always reserves the first couple of tables near the front. They loved the attention they got here and liked being able to mingle with the crowd.

The farther we get inside, I'm able to spot Brix and Ivy standing near the stage, and Madden isn't too far from them. He's built like a linebacker and is impossible to miss.

When we were in high school, the coaches didn't stop hounding him to join the team. He never had any interest in sports. At least not playing. His passion has always been music. Even when we were younger, he would turn anything and everything into a set of drums.

"You're here," Ivy cheers when the crowd parts. She crashes into me, pulling me into a hug.

Ivy's been my best friend since our days back in middle school. She always has my back, and I'll always have hers. When I found out Brix, her boyfriend and the lead singer, had made a bet with Tysin, I made it my mission to torture him.

He came to his senses and fought through hell to win her back, but she didn't make it easy on him, that's for sure.

Ivy was offered a job at *Mayhem Magazine* right after college. It's perfect for her since they're allowing her to travel with Brix on the road during the band's tour.

She will have the chance to do what she loves while also supporting his dream.

Their tour, Wreak Some Havoc, is big for them. Not only because they're headlining for the first time but also because most of their shows have sold out.

"I wish you were coming out on the road with me," she mutters against my ear. "What am I gonna do stuck on a bus full of smelly guys for three months?"

She pulls back, wearing a beaming smile on her face.

"You'll have to meet up with us at some of their shows, though. It'll be fun."

Madden sneaks in. "Congratulations, sis." He grunts, pulling me into a side hug. I practically disappear under his muscular arm.

The contrast between the two of us is almost laughable. He stands over a foot taller than me with arms the size of my head.

He slings his arm around my shoulders, pretending to put me in a chokehold. I playfully elbow him in the side before he finally releases me.

"All right, all right." He pushes me back. "Be careful before you take me out and I'm not able to have kids of my own one day."

"Lord help us all," I joke, shaking my head.

"Yo, Madden!" Brix hollers from a few feet away, nodding toward the stage.

"I'm gonna get stuff set up real quick, then I'll be back." He claps me on the shoulder. "I'm proud of you. At least one of us went to college. Pops can be happy with that, right?"

He chuckles, flashing me a wink as he backs away from us and turns to head toward the stage with the guys.

I notice the new guy Madden told me about is tuning his guitar, nodding his head along to the music. Tysin, thankfully, is nowhere in sight.

Canon comes up behind me, wrapping his arm around my waist.

"I'm goin' to grab us some drinks. I'll be right back."

I nod, running my hand over his forearm, and tilt my head up to give him a quick kiss before he disappears.

"I've missed having you at the shows with me," Ivy shouts. It's hard to hear over the music and the sounds of laughter and conversation booming around us.

If I'm being honest, I miss coming to them too. I love watching the guys play, even if it's different now.

"I do too," I say. She wraps her arm around my shoulders, and we sway back and forth to Three Doors Down.

It's been a while since we've hung out, so we use the few minutes we have with just the two of us to catch up. She tells me about how her new job is going and about the tour. They are only a few days away from leaving.

I'm still waiting for the day when Brix proposes. It's only a matter of time before it happens, but they're enjoying their time just the two of them while they can.

"What about you?" She rests her head on her palm. "What's next for you?"

There's a smug look on her face, almost as if she's keeping a secret, and she's bursting at the seams to tell me.

She reaches her hand across the table between us, stopping me midsentence, and tilts her head, signaling to something behind me. When I glance over my shoulder, my eyes land on Canon.

I spin on my heels to face him when he drops to his knee in front of me. All the oxygen is sucked out of my lungs in one quick move.

The music stops, and the crowd turns to face us, the noise level dropping with them. I slap my hand over my mouth, my eyes widening as I stare down at him.

Everything moves in slow motion from there. He holds out the black box in his hand, wearing a beaming smile on his face. He turns his hat backward. Something about that melts me every time he does. The sight of him, kneeling in front of me with the happiness radiating off him, grabs ahold of me.

How could I not want to spend every day for the rest of my life with him?

The energy in the room shifts, urging me to look up. It's almost as if I could feel the heat of Tysin's gaze, but I immediately regret it the moment I do.

My eyes lock on his. His face, his expression, is unreadable. Stoic. Emotionless.

I shake myself out of those thoughts, turning my attention back to Canon. I take a step toward him and bend forward, unable to hear him over the loud cheers and yelps of excitement erupting around us.

"I love you," I whisper against his mouth.

When I pull back, he smiles and presses another quick kiss against my lips.

"Then marry me?"

When Ivy asked me what was next, this is what I want. Canon. He's my future and the person I want to spend my life with.

I may not have a job waiting for me or all the next steps figured out, but I know I want all of it with him.

"Yes." I grin, nodding enthusiastically.

When he stands and wraps his arms around me, his lips crash against mine in a hard kiss. When I close my eyes, letting myself soak in the moment, I see Tysin's face.

Nothing betrays you more than your own mind.

CHAPTER TWO

TYSIN

"Get your shit together, man!" I snarl.

We've been practicing for almost two hours, preparing for our tour. I'm already sick of this new kid.

A Rebels Havoc has had an incredible run for the past two years. We went out on the road last summer with High Octane, and it was the big break we needed. We had labels pounding down our door, wanting a chance to talk to us.

One approached us with an offer we simply couldn't refuse.

Except it came with terms, terms I wasn't too pleased with, like adding a second guitarist to our lineup.

I was ready to wave my middle finger in the air and tell them to stick their contract up their ass.

I didn't, though.

As much as it felt like a dick smack to the face, this is everything I've been dreaming of since I was thirteen years old. It was my final *fuck you* to my mom and everyone in Carolina Beach who ever doubted me.

My love for music and my determination to see us go big won out. If all I have to do is deal with him, I'll grit my teeth and sign on the dotted line.

I still hate how it feels like all my hard work, my dream, was being handed over to him on a silver platter. He doesn't have the respect to appreciate what he's been given.

"Chill out, man!" Brix grunts under his breath.

He notices me take a step toward Trey. Pushing between us, he shoves me on the chest, attempting to calm me down.

"Chill? How would you feel if after you spent hours on lyrics, perfecting your vocals, some kid came in and re-wrote them all?"

Brix understood. We were one and the same. Cut from the same damn cloth.

Madden, on the other hand, is the voice of reason. The calm to our chaos. Whereas I had no filter and zero tolerance for bullshit.

The tension and frustration thrum through me. Brix mutters under his breath to calm down. We're crowded into the small space of our practice studio. It's our second home, the place we've used all those years.

Only now, it's starting to feel like we're crammed into a pressure cooker.

One word and we're all about to explode.

"He's right," Brix says, agreeing with me. He turns, pushing his hand against my chest. His eyes bounce over to Trey, then back to me. "We've busted our ass for the past six months, so we don't need you comin' in here and changing shit right before we leave on tour."

Trey scoffs, rolling his eyes.

"Whatever you say." He holds his hands up, shaking his head. "I didn't realize when I joined that I was gonna be stripped of my balls too. If you want to keep playing out of rhythm, more power to ya."

"Maybe we should call it a day," Madden suggests from behind his drums. His shirt is drenched, and beads of sweat drip down his face.

"Good idea. Tysin needs to go home and take some fuckin' Midol," Brix quips, crossing the room to swipe his bottle of water.

Trey joins in, a smirk stretching across his face.

"Fuck you and you," I jest, pointing at both of them.

We were all in bad moods before we even rolled in here. The truth is, we don't have time to mess around. Our tour starts in less than a week. We came back home to enjoy some downtime before we hit the road.

I was fine with wrapping up for the day. Everything about the past twenty-four hours has me ready to hit Whiskey Barrel for a beer and find someone to take back to my place.

"I need to get home and shower. We have that thing over at your parents' at six," Brix says, taking a large gulp

My eyes bounce over to Madden's, confusion furrowing my brow.

"What thing?" This is the first I've heard of anything going on.

"His parents are throwing a surprise engagement party for Kyla and Canon."

Brix's gaze lingers on me for a moment, trying to gauge my reaction.

As if witnessing it wasn't enough, I saw pictures plastered all over social media this morning.

Yeah, we had a fling. It wasn't anything serious, but it hadn't ended well. Not to mention, she was livid when she found out about the bet between me and Brix and how it hurt Ivy in the process.

She made it clear how much she hates me. Which is fine with me. I don't have any plans to try to change her mind.

In fact, the more she hates me, the easier it is for us to stay the hell away from each other.

Everything about being in CB has me wishing I could leave on tour now. It's only a matter of time before my mom catches wind we're in town. She'll come sniffing around, looking for a handout like she always does. As soon as she heard about our record deal, she was blowing up my phone to the point I blocked her number.

If she thinks for a second I'm giving her a dime, she's outta her damn mind.

Living in LA allowed me to distance myself from this part of my life. I'm ready to hit the road and do the same. With everyone chirping about Kyla's engagement, it couldn't come soon enough.

"You can come by if you want," Madden adds.

He has no idea about my history with his sister. We all knew if he did, it wasn't gonna go over well. He made it clear growing up that dating his sister was off-limits.

Probably because he knew Brix and I weren't the relationship type.

Guess he was wrong about Brix.

It wasn't worth the fight anyway. I got what I wanted out of our time together. The past is better left in the past.

"Nah, man. I think I'm gonna head home, have a few beers, and call it a night."

Madden stands, reaching into his pocket, and pulls out his phone. His brow furrows, a frown appearing on his face at whoever's calling. Brix and Trey are too busy talking about one of the songs we practiced today to notice.

He waves his hand at them, motioning with his finger over his mouth to be quiet before he answers the call.

"Hey, Harper, we're doing good. We just wrapped up a practice session now."

"Yeah, they're all still here. What's going on?"

What the hell is the owner of the record label calling Madden for? Especially so close to the start of our tour.

I pick up on the panic laced in his words, putting me on edge. My eyes bounce from Madden over to Brix. He steps away from Trey, folding his arms and tilting his head forward to listen in.

Madden nods, running his hand over his jaw, his gaze burning holes into my hardwood floors.

"What does this mean on such short notice?" he asks.

Brix flicks his eyes over to me, and I grit my teeth.

"Well, I think I know someone who could help us out. I'd have to talk to her. It's my sister. She graduated from college earlier this month with a degree in business management. While she doesn't have experience in managing a tour, she's been around the band since we started. She knows the ins and outs of what goes on behind the scenes. Plus, I trust her."

What the fuck is he talking about?

"Yeah, I'll see her here in an hour or so. I'll talk to her about it then. What is our backup plan if this doesn't pan out?"

His eyes widen, and he nods his head. I don't want to know her response but judging by the concern on his face, it's not good.

"We'll figure it out. We'll make it happen."

His words were confident and reassuring, but I know Madden. The dread on his face and the tension coiling in his body is anything but relaxed.

He ends the call, and his shoulders slouch in a heavy sigh.

"What was that all about?" Brix asks.

"The tour manager they hired fell through. Family emergency. We're less than a week away, making it hard to find a replacement."

"What's that fuckin' mean?" Brix barks, voicing what we're all thinking.

"She couldn't say, just wanted to let us know. I told her I'd talk to Kyla. She's the only person I could think of who could help us on short notice."

Madden scrubs his hand over his face, and my body goes rigid at the thought.

Three months stuck on a tour bus with Kyla?

Someone hand me a fuckin' beer now because I'm gonna need it.

BOOKS BY BROOKE

A Rebels Havoc Series

Brix
Sins of a Rebel
Tysin
Trey
Madden

Men of Blaze

Personal Foul
Reckless Rebound (Cocky Hero Club)

Tattered Heart Duet

Torn
Tattered

A Heart's Compass Series

Where I Found You
Lost Before You
Until I Found You
Now That I Found You
Where You Belong

Standalones (In order of publication)

Wild Irish

Learn more and purchase your copy at:
www.authorbrookeobrien.com/booksbybrooke

PLAYLIST

(Brooke's writing inspiration mixed in with Brix and Ivy's favorites.)

I Hate Everything About You by Three Days Grace
Gives You Hell by The All-American Rejects
Numb by Linkin Park
Say Something by A Great Big World
Unsteady by X Ambassadors
In the End by Linkin Park
Here Without You by 3 Doors Down
Scars by Papa Roach
Highway to Hell by AC/DC
Bad At Love by Halsey

Listen to the Playlist on Spotify at:
www.authorbrookeobrien.com/brix

ABOUT BROOKE

USA Today Bestselling author Brooke O'Brien writes steamy and swoon-worthy new adult romances. She's best known for her sports and rock star romances.

Brooke believes a love worth having is worth fighting for, and she brings this into her stories where her characters risk it all for love.

When she isn't writing or falling in love with a new book boyfriend, you can find her spending time with her family, cheering on her favorite sports teams, listening to ASMR, or binge-watching the latest true crime documentary. She loves rockin' a comfy hoodie with leggings and believes the best days include a good nap.

Brooke loves connecting with readers and hopes you'll join her on her social pages or reader group to stay in touch. To follow Brooke and join her newsletter, visit authorbro okeobrien.com/follow.

ACKNOWLEDGMENTS

My Boys – I love you more than anything on this earth. Everything I do is for our family.

Mom, Gram, & Ash – Thanks for always being supportive of this journey. You've pushed me to go after everything I want in life. Love you!

To my AMAZING beta readers – Kristen, Candyce, Ana, Danielle, and Cheryl. Thank you for reading Brix & Ivy's story before anyone else, for your honest feedback, and helping me make their story better. I'm so grateful for you! <3

My Rebels Babes – I flove being able to connect with all of you in my Reader Group. I feel like I've found a place where I can share with you my triumphs and crazy ideas, as well as catching up with you about everything going on in our daily lives. I'm so grateful to have all your support.

To my Rebel Release Team, thank you for being a part of this one. I'm excited to hear what you think of Brix.

Kristen – You keep it real with me, always! It's what I love about you. Thanks for riding my ass when I need it, but also reminding me to be patient with myself too. Girl, you're stuck with me now! LOL! Not even sorry about it either.

Candyce – You've helped me in so many ways since we've first met. I'm so appreciative for all you do behind the scenes. Thank you for everything!

Kim Cermak – Thank you SO much for everything! You've been a good friend to me and have supported me in so many ways throughout this journey. We make a heck of a team!

Kate Jessop – What would I do without you? I don't want to find out. Thank you for being there for me when I need to brainstorm an idea or tell me it's going to be okay when I need to hear it.

My editor, Roxane LeBlanc. I always enjoy working with you. Thank you for being honest, patient, and so very helpful to me.

My proofreader, Julie Deaton. You have a fantastic eye for detail, and I appreciate all your help in getting this book polished off. Thank you for everything!

Dee Garcia with Black Widow Designs, you are so incredibly talented and blow me away with your work. Thank you for designing the most beautiful cover.

To Jennifer with Wildfire Marketing, thank you for your support and helping me promote my work. I'm forever grateful!

Lastly, to all the fantastic bloggers and authors who have

shown me support throughout this journey. I hope you know how grateful I am for every one of you.

COPYRIGHT

This is a work of fiction. Names, characters, places and incidents either are the product of the author's imagination or are used fictitiously. Any resemblance to persons, living or dead, business establishments, events, or locales is entirely coincidental. The author acknowledges the trademarked status and trademark owners of various products referenced in this work of fiction, which has been used without permission. The publication/use of these trademarks is not authorized, associated with or sponsored by the trademark owners.

For information on subsidiary rights, please contact Tattered Ink Publishing at www.authorbrookeobrien.com.

Cover Art by Black Widow Designs

Cover Photo © Shutterstock
Edited by Rox LeBlanc, Roxs Reads
Proofread by Julie Deaton, Deaton Author Services
Version: BMO08042023

Printed in Great Britain
by Amazon